Gustav Kobbé

Wagner's Life and Works

Vol. 1

Gustav Kobbé

Wagner's Life and Works
Vol. 1

ISBN/EAN: 9783337386740

Printed in Europe, USA, Canada, Australia, Japan

Cover: Foto ©Raphael Reischuk / pixelio.de

More available books at **www.hansebooks.com**

WAGNER'S LIFE

AND

WORKS.

VOL. I. {
BIOGRAPHY, * * *
BAYREUTH ECHOES,
WRITINGS, * * * *
CRITICS, * * * *
OPERAS. * * * *
}

BY

GUSTAV KOBBÉ.

SECOND EDITION

New York:

G. SCHIRMER.

1896.

— TO —

CAROLYN WHEELER KOBBÉ.

PREFACE.

THESE volumes are the outgrowth of an analysis of "The Ring of the Nibelung," published as a pamphlet three years ago. It having passed through four editions, a fifth enlarged and illustrated edition was published last fall. The success of this having proved its usefulness to the lay musical public, the present volumes were undertaken. They make pretense to nothing more than giving as much information as the lay reader would care for concerning Wagner's life and works. For this reason technical expressions and discussions have been avoided.

The biography is based on Dannreuther's admirable story of Wagner's life in Grove's "Dictionary of Music and Musicians" (Macmillan & Co.), and upon the "Correspondence of Wagner and Liszt" (Scribner & Welford), many extracts from which are given, so that much of the story of the most interesting years of Wagner's life is told in his own words. That capital book, "Art Life and Theories of Richard Wagner" (Henry Holt & Co.), by Edward L. Burlingame, now the scholarly editor of *Scribner's Magazine*, was also consulted.

In preparing the analyses of the music dramas the writings of Von Wolzogen and Heintz were found valuable aids.

GUSTAV KOBBÉ.

SHORT HILLS, ESSEX Co., N. J., October, 1890.

CONTENTS.

ILLUSTRATIONS.

BIOGRAPHY.

HOUSE OF WAGNER'S BIRTH.

BIOGRAPHY.

RICHARD WAGNER was born at Leipsic, May 22, 1813. His ancestors were natives of Saxony. His grandfather, Gottlob Wagner, who died in 1795, held a subordinate position in the city government. His grandmother, Johanna Wagner, was the daughter of a principal of one of the public schools. Their eldest son, Carl Friedsohn, father of Richard, was born at Leipsic in 1770. He was clerk to the city police court and a man of good education. During the French occupation of Leipsic he was, owing to his knowledge of French, made chief of police. He was fond of poetry and had a special love for the drama, taking part in amateur theatricals, which were given in a building especially set apart for that purpose by the Government. In 1798 he married Johanna Rosina Bertz. The ninth child of this union was Wilhelm Richard Wagner.

He was born in a quaint old house in the Brühl, now No. 88. The date of his birth is inscribed on a white marble slab between the first and second stories. The house is now an inn called the White

and Red Lion (Der weisse und rothe Löwe). Five
months after Richard's birth his father died of an
epidemic fever brought on by the carnage during
the battle of Leipsic, October 16, 18 and 19, 1813. In
1815, his widow, whom he had left in most straitened circumstances, married Ludwig Geyer, born
January 21, 1780, at Eisleben, an actor, a playwright
and a portrait painter. One of his plays, "The
Slaughter of the Innocents," achieved considerable
success. On the occasion of Wagner's sixtieth birthday, in 1873, at Bayreuth, a private performance of
this play was given, much to his delight. Wagner
honored Geyer's memory and always spoke of him
most affectionately. At the time Wagner's mother
married Geyer he was a member of the Court
Theatre at Dresden, and thither the family removed.
Wagner says that Geyer wanted to make a painter of
him, but "I was very unhandy at drawing. I had
learned to play on the piano 'Uebt immer Treu und
Redlichkeit' and the 'Jungfernkranz" from 'Der
Freischütz,' two pieces which were then quite new.
The day before his death, September 30, 1821, I was
playing these in an adjoining room, and I heard him
saying to my mother, 'Do you think he might have a
gift for music?'" Coming out of the death room
Wagner's mother gave a message from her dead husband to each one of the children, saying to Richard:
"Of you he wanted to make something." "From
this time on," says Wagner, "I always had an idea
that I was destined to amount to something in this
world."

When he was nine years old Richard was sent to the Kreuzschule in Dresden. He proved himself an excellent Greek scholar, but was not at all proficient in Latin. He made, however, quite a little reputation at the school as a writer of German verses. Once the boys were asked to write some lines commemorative of the death of a schoolfellow, and Wagner's verses received the distinction of being printed after the excision of much that was bombastic. He was then eleven years old. That he aimed high may be judged from the fact that he began sketching tragedies modeled upon German imitations of the Greek. He also attempted to translate, metrically, *Romeo's* monologue. He states naively that he did this in order to learn English. He was such an enthusiastic admirer of Shakespeare that at the age of fourteen he began a grand tragedy, of which he himself says that it was a jumble of " Hamlet " and " Lear." So many people died in the course of it that their ghosts had to return in order to keep the fifth act going. Musically he was deeply affected by Weber's compositions. He knew the airs from " Der Freischütz " by memory, and played the overture " with the most horrible fingering." " My teacher," he adds, " once overheard me doing this, and pronounced that I would come to nothing. He was right; I have never in my life learned to play the piano." When Weber, as he often did, passed the house on his way to the theatre, Richard would watch him with feelings akin to religious awe.

After Geyer's death it became necessary for the

children to shift for themselves as much as possible
The eldest sister obtained a position at the Leipsic
Theatre as leading lady, and thither the mother followed with the younger members of the family,
Richard entering school there early in 1828. Owing
to the fact that he was put back a class he took a dislike to the school and the teachers, grew negligent of
his lessons, and took interest in nothing excepting his
big tragedy. At the Gewandhaus concerts he heard
for the first time several of Beethoven's symphonies
and also his music to "Egmont." Nothing would
now suit him except to write music for his own tragedy. From a circulating library he obtained a copy of
Logier's thorough bass, but did not make much progress with it. He then took lessons of Gottlieb Müller, subsequently organist at Altenburg, composed a
quartet, a sonata and an oratorio. Master and pupil
did not get along at all well together. Wagner was
too original, too self assertive to submit to Müller's
pedantry. His mind now took another literary turn.
He devoured the writings of E. T. A. Hoffmann, and
thus became acquainted when only in his sixteenth
year with material which turns up in some of his
works. Thus Hoffmann's "Serapion's Bruder" contains a story about the legendary contest of "Meistersinger" (Hoffmann's misnomer for Minnesingers)
at Wartburg (second act of "Tannhäuser"); and sundry
germs of Wagner's "Meistersinger" are to be found
in Hoffmann's "Meister Martin der Kufer von Würzburg." Ludwig Tieck's narrative poem, "Tannhäuser," was read at the same time.

From now on Wagner so neglected his studies that they may be said to have practically ceased. He wrote overtures for grand orchestra and dabbled in politics. When he was seventeen years old one of his overtures was performed between two of the acts at the theatre. He says of it:

"I chose, to aid the clearer comprehension of anyone who should study the parts, to write them in three different inks—the stringed instruments red, the reed instruments green and the brass instruments black. Beethoven's ninth symphony was to be a mere Pleyel's sonata beside this wonderfully composed overture. This was the culminating point of my absurdities. The public was fairly puzzled by the persistence of the drum player, who had to give a loud beat every four bars from beginning to end. People grew impatient, and finally laughed at the thing as a joke."

After entering the University of Leipsic in 1830 he had the good luck to find as a master Theodore Weinlig, cantor at the Thomas-schule, who was not only a fine musician but a man of kindly and sympathetic disposition. As late as 1877 Wagner spoke feelingly of his teacher's memory, using words which may well bear repetition as being a criticism on the routine method of technical musical instruction which is still too prevalent:

"Weinlig had no special method. He was simply clear headed and practical. You cannot teach composition. You may show how music gradually came to be what it is, and thus guide a young man's judg-

ment. This, however, is historical criticism and cannot directly result in practice. The most you can do
is to point to some working example, some particular piece, set the pupil a similar task and correct his
work. This is what Weinlig did for me. He chose
a piece, generally something of Mozart's, and then
pointed out its construction and relative length, the
balance of its sections, principal modulations, the
number and character of its themes and the general
character of the movement. My task then was :
'You shall write about so many bars, divided into so
many sections, with modulations to correspond so
and so ; the themes may be so many and of such and
such a character.' Similarly he would set contra-
puntal exercises, canons, fugues. After a minute
analysis of an example he gave simple directions how
I was to go to work.

"But the true lesson consisted in his patient and
careful inspection of what had been written. With
infinite kindness he would put his finger on some
defective bit and explain the why and wherefore of
the alterations he thought desirable. I readily saw
what he was aiming at and soon managed to please
him. He dismissed me, saying : 'You have learned
to stand on your own legs.' My experience of forty
years has led me to think that music should be
taught all round on such a simple plan. With singing, playing, composing, take it at whatever stage
you like, there is nothing so good as a proper example and careful correction of the pupil's attempts
to follow that example."

This course of instruction continued for about six months, the only known results of it being a sonata in B flat in four movements, opus 1, and a polonaise in D for four hands, opus 2. These were published by Breitkopf & Härtel and betray nothing of the future master, being in the usual form and devoid of any of those harmonic progressions so characteristic of Wagner at a later period. A fantasia in F sharp minor remains in manuscript.

During this time he led a pretty rapid life, after the manner of many German students, but a reaction soon set in and music was again taken up with earnestness. In 1830 he transcribed Beethoven's ninth symphony for the piano, and in 1831 he offered his services to the Bureau de Musique as a proof reader and an arranger. A writer says of him at this time : "I doubt if there ever was a young musician who knew Beethoven's works more thoroughly than Wagner did in his eighteenth year. The scores of the overtures and larger instrumental compositions he had copied for himself. He went to sleep with the quartets, he sang the songs and whistled the concertos, for his piano playing was never of the best." In 1831 he wrote two overtures, one of which was performed December 25 of the same year. Both remain in manuscript. In 1832, at the age of nineteen, he went to Vienna with the view of securing the performance of a symphony in four movements (C major). He was unsuccessful, but it was brought out after a trial performance at a concert in Leipsic, January 10, 1833. Wagner has an interesting anecdote to tell of this work. In 1834 or 1835 he presented the score to Mendelssohn, or rather thrust it upon him, hoping to secure another performance for it. Mendelssohn, however, never mentioned the matter again and Wagner was too proud to do so. After Mendelssohn's death all inquiry and search for the manuscript proved fruitless, but in 1872 there was discovered in Dresden an old trunk which had been left there by Wagner during the political disturbances of 1849. Among other musical odds and ends there was found an almost complete set of the orchestral parts of the missing symphony. From these a new score was compiled, and on Christmas Eve, 1882, after nearly half a century from the date of its composition and less than two months before the composer's death, a private performance of the symphony was given at Venice, Wagner conducting. The symphony has no value beyond that which attaches to it as a youthful work of a man who afterward became great.

During Wagner's sojourn in Prague in the summer of 1832 he wrote the libretto of an opera, " The Marriage," which had a highly tragic plot. When he returned to Leipsic he began to write the music for it, a septet, winning the approval of Weinlig. But the verses were destroyed, as his sister Rosalie disapproved of the plot. An autograph copy of the introduction, chorus and septet presented by him to the Würzburger Musikverein is still extant. In 1833, at the age of twenty, Wagner began his career as a professional musician. His elder brother Albert was engaged as tenor, actor and stage manager at the Würzburg Theatre. A position as chorus master being offered to him, he accepted it, though his salary was a pittance of 10 florins a month. However, the experience was valuable. He was able to profit by many useful hints from his brother, the Musikverein performed several of his compositions, and his duties were not so arduous but that he found time to write the words and music of an opera in three acts entitled " The Fairies ''—first performed in June, 1888, five years after Wagner's death, at Munich. In the autumn of 1834 he was called to the conductorship of the opera at Magdeburg. He wrote some fugitive pieces there that were successful and also produced an opera, " Das Liebesverbot '' (" Love Veto ''), based on Shakespeare's " Measure for Measure.'' The theatre at Magdeburg was, however, always on the ragged edge of bankruptcy. The manager had a pleasant habit of vanishing whenever pay day came around, and during the spring of 1836 matters became so bad that it was evident the theatre must soon close. Finally only twelve days were left for the rehearsing and the performance of his opera. The result was that the production went completely to pieces, singers forgetting their lines and music, and a repetition which was announced could not come off because of a free fight behind the scenes between two of the principal singers, which Wagner describes in the following amusing passage in his autobiographical sketch :

" All at once the husband of my prima donna (the impersonator of *Isabella*) pounced upon the second tenor, a very young and handsome fellow (the singer of my *Claudio*), against whom the injured spouse had long cherished a secret jealousy. It seemed that the prima donna's husband, who had from behind the curtain inspected with me the composition of the audience, considered that the time had now arrived when, without damage to the prospects of the theatre, he could take his revenge on his wife's lover. *Claudio* was so pounded and belabored by him that the unhappy individual was compelled to retire to the dressing room with his face all bleeding. *Isabella* was informed of this, and rushing desperately toward her furious lord, received from him such a series of violent cuffs that she forthwith went into spasms. The confusion among my personnel was now quite boundless ; everybody took sides with one party or the other, and everything seemed on the point of a general fight. It seemed as if this unhappy evening appeared to all of them precisely calculated for a final settling up of all sorts of fancied insults. This much was evident, that the couple who had suffered under the 'love veto' (Liebesverbot) of *Isabella's* husband were certainly unable to appear on this occasion."

The writing and composition of the opera had occupied much of his leisure time during 1834, '35 and '36. He left Magdeburg for Leipsic with nothing to live on excepting the interest on his debts, while the principal grew at a rapid rate. Finding nothing to do at Leipsic, he went, after a short interim at Berlin, to Königsberg. There he arranged a concert at the theatre which resulted in his appointment as conductor, and the first thing he did after the appoint-

ment was to add to his debts by marrying the "leading lady," Wilhelmina, or Minna, Planer. During his
sojourn at Königsberg he wrote an overture, "Rule
Britannia." The overture "Columbus" was played at
one of the concerts which preceded his appointment
as conductor. He chafed under the provincial rule
of the little theatre and yearned for a broader field for
his activity. Hoping to gain a foothold in Paris, he
sent a sketch for an opera in four acts, "Die hohe
Braut," to Scribe, who, however, took no notice of it.
He was, however, soon relieved of the necessity of sub-
mitting to the Königsberg routine. The director of
the opera followed in the footsteps of his Magdeburg
colleague, and declared himself bankrupt. Wagner was
not long idle. He received notice of his appointment
as conductor and of the engagement of his wife and
sister at the theatre about to be opened at Riga, on
the Russian side of the Baltic.

His sojourn in Riga is important, for it marks the
period when he began the composition of his first
great success, "Rienzi." He completed the libretto
during the summer of 1838, and began the music in
the autumn, and when his contract terminated in the
spring of 1839 the first two acts were finished. In
July, accompanied by his wife and a huge Newfound-
land dog, he boarded a sailing vessel for London, at
the port of Pillau, his intention being to go from London to Paris. "I shall never forget the voyage," he
says. "It was full of disaster. Three times we nearly
suffered shipwreck, and once were obliged to seek safety
in a Norwegian harbor. * * * The legend of the

'Flying Dutchman' was confirmed by the sailors, and the circumstances gave it a distinct and characteristic color in my mind. We stopped eight days in London to recover from the trying effects of the voyage. I was interested above all things in the aspect of the town and the Houses of Parliament ; of the theatres I saw nothing." Dannreuther says concerning this stay in London : " They lodged for a night at the Hoop and Horseshoe, 10 Queen street, Tower Hill, still existing ; then stayed at the King's Arms boarding house, Great Compton street, Soho ; from which place the dog disappeared, and turned up again after a couple of days, to his master's frantic joy. Wagner's accurate memory for localities was puzzled when he wandered about Soho with the writer in 1877 and failed to find the old house. Mr. J. Cyriax, who has zealously traced every step of Wagner's in London in 1839, '55 and '77, states that the premises have been pulled down."

From London Wagner went to Bologna, where he remained four weeks, becoming acquainted with Meyerbeer, whose influence he considered it important to gain. Armed with letters of introduction from him, he set out for Paris, where he arrived in September, 1839, and remained until April 7, 1842, from his twenty-sixth to his twenty-ninth year. This Parisian sojourn was one of the bitter experiences of his life. He at times actually suffered from cold and hunger, and was obliged to do a vast amount of the most uncongenial kind of hack work. He lodged in a remote quarter, Rue de la Tonnellerie, in a house which is

said to have been the birthplace of Molière. Meyerbeer's letters insured him polite attention, but nothing more. He could not have " Rienzi " performed,
but his "Liebesverbot" was accepted for the Re-
naissance. Elated by his prospects of artistic and
financial success, Wagner at once moved into better
quarters in the Rue de Helder, but on the very day of
his moving the theatre failed and was closed. In
these straits he even offered himself as a chorus
singer at a small Boulevard theatre, but could not
obtain the position for lack of voice. He composed
a number of songs, among them the " Two Gren-
adiers," into which he introduced the " Marseillaise."
This song was not a very satisfactory composition,
but three others, " Dors, Mon Enfant," " Mignonne "
and " Attente " are gems, and one can account for
the refusal of publishers to bring them out only on
the ground of their merit. " Mignonne" got into
print in the pages of a French periodical, and Wagner
received a few francs for it. It and the two others
appeared as a supplement to Lewald's " Europa,"
1841-42.

February 4, 1840, he finished the score of the first
truly Wagnerian work. This was revised and published fifteen years later under the title of " A Faust
Overture." He conceived it after hearing a rehearsal
of Beethoven's ninth symphony at the conservatory
in the winter of 1839. In a certain sense it is an autobiographical piece of music, for it reflects the lone-
liness and wretchedness of his life and character.
He had intended to write a complete " Faust " sym-

phony, of which this was to be the first movement.
It had a trial performance at Dresden, July 22, 1844,
but was laid on the shelf until 1855, when a revised
version was published. Liszt, who afterward became
his guardian angel, he met in Paris in 1840, but Wagner was not particularly attracted by his personality
at that time. Liszt was then at the height of his
fame as an artist, and possibly Wagner was irritated
at his facile success. He said of him at that time:
"If Liszt ever reaches a better world he will probably treat the angels to a *Fantaisie sur le Diable*," a
dig not only at Liszt, but also at Meyerbeer. November 19, 1840, he completed the score of "Rienzi,"
and on December 4 forwarded it to Von Luttichau,
the director of the Opera at Dresden. While waiting
the result he contributed to the newspapers and did
all kinds of musical drudgery for Schlesinger, the
music publisher, making arrangements even for the
cornet à piston. In February, 1841, his overture
"Columbus" was performed at the annual concert
given by Schlesinger to the subscribers to his *Gazette*.
It was the only performance of one of Wagner's
works at Paris during his first residence there. The
score and parts were lost upon this occasion, and
have not been found. Previous to this, during the
summer of 1840, Meyerbeer had returned to Paris,
and through him Wagner secured a personal introduction to the director of the Opera, Pillet. Wagner
submitted sketches for a libretto to "The Flying
Dutchman," which were accepted.

Pillet, however, wanted to have another composer

furnish the music, and offered Wagner a sum for his sketches. The matter remained in abeyance until the spring of 1841, when Wagner took refuge from his creditors in the suburbs at Meudon. There he happened to learn that his "Flying Dutchman" sketches had been handed to Paul Foucher for versification, and as he saw no way of protecting his rights, he finally accepted £20 as his compensation. "Le Vaisseau Fantôme," libretto by Foucher and Revoil, on Wagner's plan, but with sundry interpolations of the conventional sort, music by Pierre Louis Phillippe Dietsche (chorus master and subsequently conductor at the Opera), was performed November 9, 1842.

This "Vaisseau Fantôme" proved a phantom ship indeed, as it soon disappeared from the stage. After selling the sketches, Wagner immediately wrote his own version and set it to music, finishing the entire score, excepting the overture, in seven weeks. "After a nine months' interruption of any kind of musical production," he writes, "I had to work myself back into the musical atmosphere. I hired a piano, but when it had come I walked about it in an agony of anxiety; I feared to find that I was no longer a musician. I began with the sailors' chorus and the spinning song; everything went easily, fluently, and I fairly shouted for joy as I felt through my whole being that I was still an artist. In seven weeks the opera was finished."

[The overture he could not compose until after an interim of two months' drudgery. He says : "I offered the book of the 'Dutchman' to the directors of Mu-

nich and Leipsic ; they refused it as being unsuitable
for Germany. I, poor fellow, had supposed it suitable
only for Germany." At Berlin it was accepted at
Meyerbeer's instigation, but with small prospect of
immediate performance. While casting about for
other subjects, he was attracted by the story of the
conquest of Apulia and Sicily by Manfred, son of the
Emperor Frederick II., and he sketched a libretto,
"The Saracens," in which a prophetess, Manfred's
half sister by an Arabian mother, leads the Saracens
to victory, which results in Manfred's coronation. He
never set it to music, as Mme. Devrient, to whom he
showed it some years later, disapproved of it. It
chanced that a simple and popular version of the story
of " Tannhäuser " came into his hands. It made a
deep impression on him. He was familiar with the
subject from his youthful reading, to which reference
has been made. He had also learned that Weber had
planned an opera on the subject. The impression
was deepened by his reading the mediæval German
poem, a copy of which was loaned to him by an acquaintance.

One of the manuscript copies of this poem introduces also the poem of " Lohengrin," and he was
thus led to the study of Wolfram von Eschenbach's
" Parzival and Titurel." " Tannhäuser " was thus the
key which opened to him the rich treasure house of
the German mediæval legends. He began the sketch
of his libretto during an excursion to the Bohemian
hills in July, 1842, and at Teplitz the preliminary
outline was completed. Meanwhile " Rienzi " had

aroused the enthusiasm of the chorus master, Herr Fischer, and of the great tenor Tichatschek, at Dresden, Tichatschek divining that the rôle was exactly suited to his robust, ringing dramatic voice. Then there was Mme. Schroeder-Devrient for the part of *Adriano*. The opera was finally produced, with Reissiger as conductor, the night of October 20, 1842, the performance beginning at 6 and ending just before midnight, to the enthusiastic plaudits of an immense audience. So great was the excitement that in spite of the late hour people remained awake to talk over the success. "We all ought to have gone to bed," relates a witness, "but we did nothing of the kind." Early the next morning Wagner appeared at the Opera House in order to make excisions from the score, which he thought its great length necessitated. But when he returned in the afternoon to see if they had been executed, the copyist excused himself by saying the singers had protested against any cuts. Tichatschek said: "I will have no cuts; it is too heavenly." The third performance was conducted by Wagner himself. After a while, however, owing to the length of the opera, it was divided into two evenings, Acts I. and II. being played the first night, Acts III., IV. and V. the second. Wagner had the same experience with it that he had with his later works. In spite of its great triumph at the place where it was produced, it was slow in making its way. It did not reach Vienna until 1871.

About the time of its production Wagner wrote his lively autobiographical sketch, which was printed in the "Zeitung für die Elegante Welt," February 1, 1843. ˥The success of " Rienzi " led the managers of the Dresden theatre to put "The Flying Dutchman " in rehearsal. It was brought out after somewhat hasty preparations January 2, 1843, with Schroeder-Devrient as *Senta*. The opera was so different from " Rienzi," its sombre beauty contrasted so darkly with the glaring, brilliant music and scenery of the latter that the audience failed to grasp it. In fact, after " Rienzi," it was a disappointment. Wagner himself considered the performance unsatisfactory ; although Schumann wrote of Devrient's *Senta* in terms of high praise, Wagner himself considered that she rather overdid the part. [The opera, however, has not only held its own, but is now considered by all reliable critics of music far superior to " Rienzi."] Spohr, on seeing the libretto, was so struck with its excellence that he at once asked for the score, and, recognizing its beauties, he straightway proceeded to produce it at Cassel, where it was given June 5, 1843. Spohr was the only musician of eminence of that day who seems to have met Wagner with anything approaching cordial appreciation. In a letter to a friend he speaks very highly of the work, yet sufficiently critically to make his praise all the more valuable, ending by saying : " I have come to the conclusion that among contemporary composers for the stage Wagner is the most gifted." Wagner states that the opera was originally intended to be performed in one act as a dramatic ballade.

Before the end of January, 1843, not long after the

success of "Rienzi," Wagner was appointed one of the conductors of the Dresden Opera. He was installed February 2. One of his first duties was to assist Berlioz at the rehearsals of the latter's concerts. Wagner's work in his new position was somewhat varied, consisting not only of conducting operas, but also music between the acts at theatrical performances and at church services. The principal operas which he rehearsed and conducted were "Euryanthe," "Freischütz," "Don Juan," "The Magic Flute," Mendelssohn's music to "The Midsummer Night's Dream," Gluck's "Armida" and "Iphigenie in Aulis." The last named was revised both as regards words and music by him, and his changes are now generally accepted. At the Pensions concerts given under his direction he produced Beethoven's ninth symphony among other works, attracting great attention by his new and poetic reading. In fact, it may be said that this symphony owes much of the progress it has made in popular favor to Wagner's enthusiasm for it. "It was worth while to make the journey from Leipsic merely to hear the recitative of the double basses," said Niels Gade. Rather an amusing remark of Wagner's has come down from his routine at the court church. Speaking of an enormous male soprano who sang there, he compared him with a "huge pudding with a voice like a cracked cornet." He became leader of the Liedertafel, a choir of male voices, and he conducted a festival of male singing societies at Dresden in July, 1843. For this he composed the "Love Feast of the Apostles," a work for three choirs of male voices, which, beginning without accompaniment, are finally heard in union with the full orchestra.

This early work in its outlines somewhat foreshadows his very latest composition, "Parsifal," though the music of the two have nothing in common. In 1844, when the remains of Weber were taken from London to Dresden, Wagner conducted the musical services at the reception of the body and the interment, December 14. Among other pieces performed was his funeral march on themes from "Euryanthe." Wagner sought Liszt's aid in the project of erecting a monument to Weber, "not," as he writes in the second of the published letters of the famous Wagner-Liszt "Correspondence," "from idleness, but because I feel convinced that the voice of a poor German composer of operas compelled to devote his lifelong labor to the spreading of his works a little beyond the limits of his province is much too feeble to be counted of importance for anything in the world."

Meanwhile he had worked arduously on "Tannhäuser," completing it April 13, 1844. But before the end of December of the same year he revised it, and it may be interesting to note that nearly a year after its production at Dresden he made a further revision of the closing scene. During the summer of 1845, even before "Tannhäuser" was produced, he was at work on new material, and he returned from Teplitz with sketches for "The Mastersingers" and "Lohengrin."

"Tannhäuser" was produced at Dresden, October

19, 1845. At first the work proved even a greater puzzle to the public than " The Flying Dutchman " had, and evoked comments which nowadays, when the opera has actually become a classic, seem ridiculous. Even Mme. Devrient, who was *Venus*, and whose scene with *Tannhäuser* in the first act fell flat, said to Wagner : " You are a genius, but you write such odd stuff one can hardly sing it." *Tannhäuser's* narrative, which foreshadows more than anything else in any of his operas his future greatness and his intense dramatic style, and is now considered one of the most inspired portions of the work, was called pointless and empty. Some people suggested that the plot of the opera should be changed so that *Tannhäuser* should marry *Elizabeth*. Wagner naturally felt isolated. He recognized that the opera was far ahead of the times ; that it was necessary to educate the public up to his art. He never for a moment considered the feasibility of lowering himself to the level of the public.

"Tannhäuser" made its way slowly. Liszt conducted the overture at Weimar, November 12, 1848, and produced the work February 16, 1849. Wiesbaden followed in 1852, Munich 1855, Berlin 1856, Vienna 1857, the Court Opera House, Vienna, November 19, 1859 ; Paris, where it made one of the most famous failures of modern times, March 13, 1861. Spohr, who brought out "Tannhäuser" at Cassel in 1853, wrote as follows : "The opera contains much that is new and beautiful, but also several disagreeable attacks on one's ears. A good deal, however, that I disliked at first, I have become accustomed to on repeated hearing. Still, the absence of rhythm and the lack of well rounded periods continue to disturb me." Mendelssohn, who, to judge from the innocent respectability of his music, its perfect form and polite melodies, seems always to have sat down to compose in his dress suit and kid gloves, could make nothing of the opera at all. [January 7, 1846, Schumann wrote from Dresden as follows: "I wish you could see 'Tannhäuser;' it contains deeper, more original and altogether a hundredfold better things than his previous operas ; at the same time a good deal that is musically trivial.] On the whole, Wagner may become of great importance and significance to the stage, and I am sure that he is possessed of the needful courage. Technical matter, instrumentation, I find altogether remarkable, beyond comparison better than formerly. Already he has finished a new text book, 'Lohengrin.'" Very different from these fairly generous words were those he wrote some years later: "Wagner is, if I am to put it concisely, not a good musician. He is wanting in the proper sense and beauty of form. Apart from the performance the music is poor, quite amateurish, empty and repelling." This sweeping criticism is not, however, nearly as cutting as Wagner's biting remark about Schumann, that he was "a clever composer, with a certain tendency toward greatness."

To Liszt, who had shown so warm an interest in his music that Wagner's first unfavorable impression of the virtuoso-composer had been effaced, Wagner had sent the score of "Tannhäuser" in March, 1846. In a letter dated the 22d of that month he says : "I have ventured to send you the scores of my 'Rienzi' and 'Tannhäuser,' and wish and hope that the latter will please you better than the former." When Liszt was rehearsing the work Wagner wrote these feeling words (January 14, 1849) : "Will you really in this evil time undergo the nuisance of tackling my 'Tannhäuser?' Have you not yet lost your courage in this arduous labor, which only in the luckiest case can be grateful?" And shortly after the performance he thanked him in these fervid sentences :

"If I have judged your beautiful action rightly, if I have understood you, I hope you will understand me, too, when, in words as brief and precise as was your action, I say to you, I thank you, dear friend ! * * * Thank God! The news from Weimar and Tichatschek's greetings and accounts have again strengthened me. I once more have courage to suffer."

Liszt's reply contained these charming words: "So much do I owe to your bold and high genius, to the fiery and magnificent pages of your 'Tannhäuser,' that I feel quite awkward in accepting the gratitude you are good enough to express with regard to the two performances I had the honor and happiness to conduct."

Wagner wrote in return: "A thousand thanks for your letter ! We are getting along nicely together ! If the world belonged to us I believe we should do something to give pleasure to the people living therein."

In 1846 Wagner began to be again harassed by

financial difficulties. Hoping after the success of
" Rienzi " that his operas would be produced at the
leading theatres, he had made a contract with a Dresden publisher to print the piano scores of " Rienzi "
and "The Flying Dutchman." To these the piano
and full score of " Tannhäuser " had been added.
The venture was not a profitable one and seems to
have left Wagner considerably in debt.   His position
in Dresden was not very congenial.   He gradually
became the leader of a small, progressive faction,
and was looked upon with suspicion by conservative
musicians and by the conservative portion of the
public, which unfortunately always forms a large
majority.   In fact, it may be said of a work of art
which strikes out in new paths that it is looked upon
as a dangerous novelty until some other more daring
novelty is brought forward and becomes the *bête noir*.
Wagner suffered a good deal from the fact that the
leading critic of Dresden, J. Schladebach, a friend of
Reissiger, was the champion of routine, and therefore made as little as possible of what he liked in
Wagner's operas and as much as possible of what he
disliked.   Thus he did Wagner considerable injury, not
only in Dresden but also in other cities with whose
newspapers he corresponded.   Wagner's personal
peculiarities were also spread before the public.   As
a result he came to be regarded even by managers who had never come in contact with him as a
difficult person to get along with, and his music, even
by those who had never heard it, was criticised as
being eccentric, and it happened in some cases that

librettos and scores which he submitted were returned unopened. In those days writers were not
treated to the pretty little printed slips which magazine editors now return with rejected manuscripts,
and composers probably fared worse. Nevertheless,
Wagner was irrepressible.

[In 1847, the year in which he first directed the
ninth symphony, he worked at "Lohengrin" as savagely as if "Tannhäuser" had been a howling success.
By early spring, 1848, the work was completed.] He
knew that it was even further in advance of the public than "Tannhäuser." The management of the .
Dresden Theatre, which had witnessed the brilliant
success of "Rienzi," and had seen "The Flying Dutchman" and "Tannhäuser" hold their own in spite of
the most virulent opposition, looked upon his new
work as altogether too risky and put off its production indefinitely.] The finale of the first act was performed on the 300th anniversary of the orchestra,
September 22, 1848, and this was all the composer
heard of the work for many years. A Berlin production of "Rienzi," October 5, 1847, did not prove a success, so that Wagner's circumstances were in no way
bettered by it. Nevertheless, we find him in 1848, in
spite of the cold shoulder which the management had
turned toward "Lohengrin," engaged upon studies
for another work. He made sketches for an opera,
with the story of the Saviour as the basis. This is interesting in view of his allegorical treatment of the
subject in "Parsifal." Then he took up the story of
Frederick Barbarossa, but turned from this to the

myth of the Nibelung. Here, then, we have away back in the autumn of 1848 the first germ of an art production which may be said to have finally gained the admiration of the civilized world, but which was not heard for nearly thirty years after Wagner first put it on paper. [Early in 1848 he made a prose version of a drama on the subject of the Nibelung myth, following it up in the autumn with "Siegfried's Death," in three acts and a prologue, written in alliterative verse, and subsequently incorporated with much new matter and many corrections in " The Dusk of the Gods." According to Dannreuther sundry germs of the music were conceived at this early period.

[Throughout these years his unsuccessful venture in publishing his scores continued to harass him. At last he turned to Liszt for aid.] These characteristic extracts from the correspondence give us insight into his life at this time. In the first he seems on the very verge of despair ; in the second he again shows that defiance of ill fortune which was one of the grandest traits of his nature: " I should once more be a *human being*, a man for whom existence would be possible, an artist who would never again in his life ask for a shilling, and would only do his work bravely and gladly. Dear Liszt, with this money you will buy me out of slavery. Do you think I am worth that sum as a serf ? " (June 23, 1848.)

"I live in a very humbled condition and without much hope. I depend on the good will of certain people. Every thought of enjoying life I have abandoned ; but—let me tell you this for your comfort—I am alive in spite of it all, and do not mean to let anyone kill me so easily."

Thinking that political changes might put an end to the routine stagnation in musical matters, Wagner joined in the revolutionary agitation of '48 and '49. June 14, 1848, he made a speech for a political club in Dresden, for which he received a reprimand from the police authorities. In May, 1849, the disturbances at Dresden reached such an alarming point that the Saxon Court fled, and Prussian troops were dispatched to quell the riot. It is said that Wagner carried a red flag and even fought on the barricades, but there is nothing to corroborate these statements. He seems, however, to have thought it advisable to flee, and he went to Weimar, where Liszt was busy rehearsing "Tannhäuser." While attending a rehearsal of this work, May 19, news was received that orders had been issued for his arrest as a politically dangerous individual. Liszt at once procured a passport and Wagner started for Paris, Liszt escorting him as far as Eisenach.

Music was at so low an ebb in Paris that Wagner was unable to make a living there. In June, 1849, he went to Zurich, where he found Dresden friends and where his wife joined him, being enabled to do so through the zeal of Liszt, who raised the money to defray her journey from Dresden.

Several of the most interesting bits from the correspondence relate to this time. The letter in which Wagner begs Liszt to forward to Mme. Wagner the money to enable her to join him in Zurich opens with the following characteristic sentences : " Are you in a good humor ?   Probably not, as you are just open- ing a letter from your plaguing spirit.   And yet it is all the world to me that you should be in a good humor just to-day, this very instant.   Fancy yourself at the most beautiful moment of your life, and look upon me cheerfully and benevolently, for I have to offer an ardent prayer."   Liszt forwarded to Mme. Wagner 100 thalers, which he procured, as he writes to Wagner, " from an admirer of ' Tannhäuser,' whom you do not know and who has specially asked me not to name him to you."

Wagner, as may be judged from the above, found himself in the most deplorable financial circumstances, and his letters about this time contain urgent appeals for assistance in order that he might have the nec- essary leisure to proceed with the composition of " Siegfried's Death," which afterward became " The Dusk of the Gods " of the " Nibelung " cycle.   The following passages from the correspondence speak for themselves :

" Oh, my friends, if you would only give me the wages of a middling mechanic, you would have pleas- ure in my undisturbed work, which should all be yours."

*   *   *   *   *   *   *

" I must commence some genuine work, or else perish ; but in order to work I want quiet and a home. With my wife and in pleasant Zurich I shall find both. I have one thing in view, and one thing I shall always do with joy and pleasure, work—*i. e.*, write operas.

For anything else I am unfit ; play a part or occupy a position I cannot, and I should deceive those whom I promised to undertake any other task."

*   *   *   *   *   *   *

"You friends must get me some small yearly allowance, just sufficient to secure for me and my wife a quiet existence in Zurich, as for the present I am not allowed to be near you in Germany. I talked to you in Weimar of a salary of 300 thalers which I would wish to ask of the Grand Duchess for my operas, alterations of the same, and the like. If perhaps the Duke of Coburg, and possibly even the Princess of Prussia, were to add something I would willingly surrender my whole artistic activity to these three protectors as a kind of equivalent, and they would have the satisfaction of having kept me free and ready for my art."

*   *   *   *   *   *   *

"The score of 'Lohengrin' will be especially useful to me, for I hope to pawn it here for some hundreds of florins, so as to have money for myself and my wife for the next few months."

*   *   *   *   *   *   *

"The question then is, how and whence shall I get enough to live ? Is my finished work, 'Lohengrin,' worth nothing ? Is the opera which I am longing to complete worth nothing ? Is it true that to the present generation these must appear as useless luxuries ? But how about the few who love these works ? Should not they be allowed to offer to the poor suf-

fering creator, not a remuneration, but the bare pos-
sibility of continuing to create ? "

*　　*　　*　　*　　*　　*　　*

" To the tradesmen I cannot apply, nor to the exist·
ing nobility—not to human princes, but to princely
men.　To work my best, my most inmost salvation,
I am not in a position to rely on merit, but on grace.
If we few in this villanous trading age are not gracious toward each other, how can we live in the name
and for the honor of art ? "

*　　*　　*　　*　　*　　*　　*

" Let someone buy my ‘Lohengrin,' skin and
bones ; let someone commission my ‘Siegfried.' I
will do it cheaply."

*　　*　　*　　*　　*　　*　　*

" If nothing else will answer, you might perhaps
give a concert ‘for an artist in distress.' Consider
everything, dear Liszt, and before all manage to send
me soon some money.　I want firewood and a warm
overcoat, because my wife has not brought my old
one on account of its shabbiness."

Liszt took up Wagner's financial cause with the
same ardor which he had displayed for his music. That
he espoused it also with considerable tact appears from
the manner in which he carried out Wagner's suggestion that he give a concert for an artist in distress.
" On my way through Hamburg," writes Liszt, " I
have yielded to numerous solicitations to conduct in
April a grand musical festival, the greater part of the
receipts of which will be devoted to the ‘Pension

Fund of Musicians,' which I founded about seven years ago. Your 'Tannhäuser' overture will, of course, figure in the program, and perhaps also, if we have sufficient time and means, the finale of the first and second act, unless you have some other pieces to propose. Kindly write on this subject to your niece, who is engaged for the whole winter at Hamburg, and ask her to come to our assistance on this occasion ; for it is my firm intention (not *avowed* or *divulged*, you understand, for there would be much inconvenience and no advantage in confiding it to friends or the public) to set aside part of the receipts for you."

At this time also Wagner gave vent in a letter to Liszt to some of the bitterness which his uncongenial position in Dresden had engendered. Referring to charges that he had shown himself ungrateful to the King of Saxony, he writes :

"One thing grieves me deeply ; it wounds me to the very bone. I mean the reproach frequently made to me that I have been ungrateful to the King of Saxony. I am wholly made of sentiment, and could never understand in the face of such a reproach why I felt no pangs of conscience at this supposed ingratitude. I have at last asked myself whether the King of Saxony has committed a punishable wrong by conferring upon me undeserved favors, in which case I should certainly have owed him gratitude for his infringement of justice. Fortunately my consciousness acquits him of any guilt. The payment of 1,500 thalers for my conducting, at his director's command, a certain number of bad operas every year was indeed excessive; but this was to me no reason for gratitude, but rather for dissatisfaction with my appointment. That he paid me nothing for the best I could do does not oblige me to *gratitude;* that when he had an opportunity of helping me thoroughly he could not or dared not help me, but calmly discussed my dismissal with his intendant, quieted me as to the dependence of my position on any act of grace."

From the time of his arrival in Zurich until 1852 he was busily engaged in writing, and a number of his important literary works date from that period. Most remarkable of these, on account of the excitement that it created when it was first published and also when it was subsequently reissued in 1869, was his "Judaism in Music." This first appeared in the *Neue Zeitschrift* under the pseudonym of K. Freigedank. Its principal effect when it first appeared was to excite the bitter and lasting hostility of a number of professional critics. When the revised and enlarged edition was issued in 1869 over a hundred replies were written, Wagner's argument being, however, entirely ignored, the charge being made and reiterated that he had disgracefully defamed rival composers because they were of Hebrew origin. As a matter of fact, however, Wagner was benefited rather than injured by the attacks made upon his essay. It made few enemies among the Hebrews, who seem to have been too intelligent to have misunderstood him and have been his admirers in large numbers; and the notoriety it gained for him in the newspapers gave his other writings, which had been sadly neglected by the public, a good sale. Wagner has been considerably criticised for an attack upon Meyerbeer made in his essay "Opera and Drama." But it may be said that Wagner wrote nothing bitter of Meyerbeer personally; he merely criticised his music as artificial and superficial. Nowadays, when Wagner towers so high above Meyerbeer, the matter is not worth discussing at any length and may be dismissed with the simple remark that, after all, Wagner's obligations to Meyerbeer were too inconsiderable to forbid him from criticising the former's music. Moreover, Wagner seems to have had good reasons to suspect Meyerbeer of instigating some of the intrigues which caused the failure of "Rienzi" in Berlin.

Shortly after the first publication of the essay Liszt wrote to Wagner : "Can you tell me under the seal of the most absolute secrecy whether the famous article on 'Judaism in Music' in Brendel's paper is by you?" Wagner, in his reply, gives his reasons for putting forth the essay : "You ask me about the 'Judenthum.' You must know that the article is by me. Why do you ask? I use a pseudonym, not from fear, but only to avoid having my personality rather than my views discussed. I felt a long repressed hatred for this Judaism, and this hatred is as necessary to my nature as gall is to the blood. An opportunity arose when their damnable scribbling annoyed me most, and so I broke forth at last. It seems to have made a tremendous impression, and that pleases me, for I really wanted only to frighten them by this method ; that they will remain the masters is as certain as that not our princes but the bankers and the Philistines are nowadays our masters. Toward Meyerbeer my position is a peculiar one. I do not hate him, but he disgusts me beyond measure. This eternally pleasant man reminds me of the most turbid, not to say most vicious, period of my life, when he pretended to be my protector; that was the period of connections and back stairs, when we are made fools of by our protectors, whom in our inmost heart we do not like."

Wagner's distinctly literary work of this period embraces also his essay on musical criticism, his "Communication to My Friends," a preface to his operatic poems "The Flying Dutchman," "Tannhäuser" and "Lohengrin," and his "Opera and Drama." The last he speaks of as a work that will be a great stout volume, of the "greatest importance" to himself and, he hopes, not without importance to others. He seems to have given his time to writing largely from lack of musical inspiration, for in the letter in which he refers to "Opera and Drama" he exclaims : "Oh! would it were spring, and that I might be once more a full blooded, poetizing musician!" ending with a lament over his straitened circumstances : "I am not very well off; care, care, nothing but care, is the funeral chant which I have to sing to every young day."

Besides his essay Wagner wrote a prose version of a drama entitled "Wieland der Schmidt," conducted concerts, gave hints regarding performances at the theatre, where one of his most enthusiastic disciples, Von Bülow, whose divorced wife he subsequently married, was one of the conductors, and also gave a reading of "Siegfried's Death" as an illustration to a lecture on the musical drama. "Wieland" he offered to Liszt as a subject for an opera; but Liszt was genius enough to realize the shortcomings of his genius, and never attempted the task. Indeed, one of the most beautiful incidents of the friendship between Wagner and Liszt was the latter's ready acknowledgment of Wagner's overshadowing greatness. At the time these relations commenced Liszt was easily the higher in popular esteem, and could have retained his pre-eminence without much, if any, effort had he chosen to do so. But with a self abnegation as rare as it is sublime (especially in art circles), he stood aside in order that the greater genius of his friend might pass to the front.

The greater portion of the Wagner-Liszt correspondence dates from the years of Wagner's exile; and at this point, when Liszt is about to inaugurate the Wagner movement in Germany by the production of "Lohengrin," it seems proper to quote the tribute of gratitude which Wagner paid to Liszt. He says: "I was again thoroughly disheartened from undertaking any new artistic scheme. Only recently I had received proofs of the impossibility of making my art intelligible to the public, and all this deterred me from beginning new dramatic works. Indeed, I thought all was at an end with my artistic creativeness. From this state of mental dejection I was

raised by a friend. By the most evident and undeni-
able proofs he made me feel that I was not deserted,
but was, on the contrary, thoroughly understood even
by those who were otherwise most distant from me ;
in this way he gave me back my most artistic confidence. This wonderful friend to me has been Franz
Liszt. I must enter a little more deeply into the
character of this friendship, which to many has
seemed paradoxical.

"I met Liszt for the first time during my first stay
in Paris and at a period when I had renounced the
hope, nay, even the wish, of a Parisian reputation,
and, indeed, was in a state of internal revolt against
the artistic life I found there. At our meeting Liszt
seemed to me the most perfect contrast to my own
being and situation. In this world, to which I had
desired to fly from my narrow circumstances, Liszt
had grown up from his earliest age and was an object of general love and admiration at a time when I
was repulsed by general coldness and want of sympathy. In consequence, I looked upon him with suspicion. I had no opportunity of disclosing my character and aspirations to him, and, therefore, his
reception of me was altogether superficial, as was
quite natural to a.man to whom every day the most
divergent impressions claimed access. My repeated
expression of this feeling was afterward reported to
Liszt just at the time when my 'Rienzi' at Dresden
attracted general attention. He was surprised to find
himself misunderstood with such violence by a man
whom he had scarcely known. I am still touched as

I recollect the repeated and eager attempts he made to change my opinion of him, even before he knew any of my works, and although acquaintance with me must have seemed without any value to him. He acted not from any artistic sympathy, but was led by the purely human wish of discontinuing a casual dishar- mony between himself and another being ; perhaps he also felt an infinitely tender misgiving of having really hurt me unconsciously. He who knows the ter- rible selfishness and insensibility in our social life, and especially in the relations of modern artists to each other, cannot but be struck with wonder, nay, delight, by the treatment I experienced from this extraor- dinary man.

" This happened at a time when it had become more and more evident that my dramatic works would have no outward success. But just when the case seemed desperate Liszt succeeded by his own energy in opening a hopeful refuge to my art. He ceased his wanderings, settled down at the small, modest Weimar, and took up the conductor's baton, after having been at home so long in the splendor of the greatest cities of Europe. At Weimar I saw him for the last time, when I rested a few days in Thuringia, not yet certain whether the threatened political prose- cution would compel me to continue my flight from Germany. The very day when my personal danger became a certainty, I saw Liszt conduct a rehearsal of my ' Tannhäuser,' and was astonished at recognizing my second self in his achievement. What I had felt in inventing this music he felt in performing it ;

what I wanted to express in writing it down he pro-
claimed in making it sound. Strange to say, through
the love of this rarest friend I gained at the moment
of becoming homeless the real home for my art,
which I had longed for and sought for always in the
wrong place.

"At the end of my last stay in Paris, when ill,
miserable and despairing I sat brooding over my
fate, my eye fell on the score of my 'Lohengrin,'
totally forgotten by me. Suddenly I felt something
like compassion that this music should never sound
from off the death pale paper. Two words I wrote
to Liszt; his answer was the news that preparations
for the performance were being made on the largest
scale the limited means at Weimar would permit.
Everything that men and circumstances could do was
done in order to make the work understood. Success
was his reward, and with this success he now approaches me, saying : 'Behold, we have come so far ;
now create us a new work that we may go still
farther.' "

Liszt brought out "Lohengrin " at Weimar, August
28, 1850, on the anniversary of Goethe's birth and the
date of the inauguration of the Herder statue. The
work was performed without cuts and before an
audience which included some of the leading musical and literary men of Germany. While the reception of "Lohengrin " did not at first differ much from
that accorded to "Tannhäuser," the performance
made a deep impression. The circumstance that
Liszt added the charm of his personality to it and

that the weight of his influence had been thrown in
its favor alone gave vast importance to the event.
Moreover, it made for Wagner friends in high places,
and it may be said that through this performance
Wagner's cause received its first great stimulus —
in fact the so-called Wagner movement may be
said to date from this production of "Lohengrin."
Wagner rightly gauged the feelings of professional
musicians when he said : "Musicians agreed to my
dabbling in poetry, poets admitted my musical at-
tainments ; I have been frequently able to arouse the
public; professional critics have always disparaged
me." A rather clever satirical remark, somewhat in
this vein, by one of his opponents may be quoted.
This man said : "To me Wagner is greater than
Schiller or Beethoven—he composes better music
than Schiller and he writes better poetry than Beethoven."

"Lohengrin" was given at Wiesbaden in 1833, and
after that made its way quite rapidly, and it has since
then held its place in Germany as the most popular
of his works, a large percentage of the female population of the Fatherland born since the production of
the opera being named after the heroine of the work.

Some highly interesting bits of the correspondence
relate to "Lohengrin" and its production. Writing
to a mutual friend from Zurich, March 20, 1849,
Wagner says :

"Liszt will shortly receive a parcel of scores, &c.,
from my wife; let him open it. The score of
'Lohengrin' I want him to try at some leisure ; it is

my last and ripest work.   As yet I have not shown it
to any artist, and therefore have not been able to
learn from anyone what impression it produces. How
curious I am to hear Liszt about it !"

Liszt was evidently not yet quite ready for a work
so advanced (for 1849) as 'Lohengrin ;' he at least
doubts the practicability of producing it.   He writes :

"The admirable score of ' Lohengrin ' has interested
me profoundly ; nevertheless I fear at the performance the *superideal* color which you have maintained
throughout.   Perhaps you will think me an awful
Philistine, dear friend, but I cannot help it."

The work, however, grew upon him.

" All the scores (excepting the overture to ' Faust ')
I sent to Zurich last week. The separation from
your ' Lohengrin ' was difficult to me. The more I
enter into its conception and masterly execution the
higher rises my enthusiasm for this extraordinary
work. Forgive my wretched pusillanimity if I still
have some doubt as to the wholly satisfactory result
of the performance."

But little over a year after Wagner had forwarded
the " Lohengrin " score to Liszt, April 21, 1850, he
penned from Paris the following pathetic appeal to
his tutelary genius :

'Dear friend, I have just been looking through the
score of my ' Lohengrin.' . I very seldom read my own
works. An immense desire has sprung up in me to
have this work performed. I address this wish to
your heart.

"Perform my ' Lohengrin ! ' *You are the only one*

to whom I could address this prayer ; to none but you I should intrust the creation of this opera ; to you I give it with perfect and joyous confidence. Perform it where you like, even if only in Weimar ; I feel certain you will procure every possible and necessary means, and they will refuse you nothing. Perform ' Lohengrin,' and let its existence be *your* work."

Notwithstanding the doubts Liszt had entertained regarding the adaptability of the work for performance, he threw himself heart and soul into the production.

"Your 'Lohengrin,'" he writes, " will be given under exceptional conditions, which are most favorable to its success. The management for this occasion spends about 2,000 thalers, a thing that has not been done in Weimar within the memory of man. The press will not be forgotten, and suitable and seriously conceived articles will appear successively in several papers. All the personnel will be put on its mettle. The number of violins will be slightly increased (from sixteen to eighteen) and a bass clarinet has been purchased. Nothing essential will be wanting in the musical material or design. I undertake all the rehearsals with piano, chorus, strings and orchestra."

Wagner at once became all activity. As well as he could from a distance he superintended the production, sending to Liszt instructions regarding many details. His letters show him to have been in excellent spirits.

"First of all," he writes from Thuny, "I have in

the inclosed treated of scenery and decorations. My drawings made for that purpose will give you great delight; I count them among the most successful creations of my genius. Where my technic forsook me you must be satisfied with the good intention, which will be clear to you from the literary explanation attached to it. The trees especially presented insuperable difficulties, and if every painter has to perspire over perspective as I have done his art is by no means an easy calling."

Nor were his letters lacking in gratitude to Liszt. Thus he writes :

"Who knows better than myself that in our dear world of the Mine and Thine, of work and payment, I am a pure luxury ? He who gives anything to me receives something quite superfluous and unnecessary in return. What do you think, who have taken such infinite pains to dispose of my works ? Much as I think of 'Lohengrin,' which you are bringing to light, I think as much and almost more of you and your terrible exertions. I know what these exertions are. When I saw you conduct a rehearsal of 'Tannhäuser' I knew at once what you were to me."

But the most important result of this "Lohengrin" production was its inspiring effect upon Wagner. It stimulated afresh his musical genius, which was in danger of stagnating through lack of artistic sympathy.

" Now," he writes, " you offer me the artistic environments which might bring 'Siegfried' to light. I demand representatives of heroes such as our stage

has not yet seen ; where are they to come from ?
Not from the air, but from the earth ; for I believe
you are in a good way to make them grow from the
earth by dint of your inspiring care. * * *
Well, then, as soon as you have produced 'Lohengrin' to your own satisfaction I shall also produce
my 'Siegfried,' but only for you and for Weimar.
Two days ago I should not have believed that I
should come to this resolution ; I owe it to you.
* * * I still feel enthusiasm for art, for its own
sake ; the music of my 'Siegfried' vibrates through
all my nerves ; it all depends upon a favorable mood,
and that you, dear friend, will procure for me.
* * * I think the devil will not get hold of me
just yet."

At the production of "Lohengrin" it was found to
occupy so much time in performance that the management addressed Wagner on the subject of "cuts," re-
questing him to make them, as he would know how to
shorten the work without doing violence to it. With
impracticable but noble faith in " Lohengrin " as it was
he refused to mutilate his work with his own hand,
writing to the director in the following characteristic
manner :

" If we yield in small and simple things—if we make
concessions to laziness and incompetence, we may
be sure that we shall soon be obliged to do the same
throughout ; in other words, that we must give up
every attempt at making a work like the present suc-
ceed. * * * You will see from this, most es-
teemed Herr Intendant, how important it is for me

not to gain toleration for my 'Lohengrin' by accommodating it to existing evils, but to secure for it a decisive success by making it conquer existing evils."

Liszt, not content with producing the work as perfectly as his own enthusiastic participation in the production would insure, wrote an elaborate and appreciative essay and labored otherwise to further Wagner's cause. Referring to the essay Wagner writes: "If I were to tell you what I felt while reading this article repeatedly and most carefully I should scarcely be able to find words. Let this suffice: I feel more than fully rewarded for my efforts, my sacrifices and my artistic struggles by recognizing the impression I have made upon you of all others. To be so fully understood was my only longing, and to have been understood is the most blissful satisfaction of that longing." He also has a fling at his unfavorable critics:

"The most terrible of all things is a German æsthetic littérateur."

Meanwhile he had found it necessary to completely remodel his plan for a music drama on the subject of the Nibelung legend. The backward evolution of this work is most interestingly described in a letter from Wagner to Liszt, dated November 20, 1851:

"In the autumn of 1848 I sketched for the first time the complete myth of the 'Nibelungen,' such as it henceforth belongs to me as my poetic property. My next attempt at dramatizing the chief catastrophe of that great action for our theatre was 'Siegfried's

Death.' After much wavering I was at last, in the autumn of 1850, on the point of sketching the musical execution of this drama, when again the obvious impossibility of having it adequately performed anywhere prevented me in the first instance from beginning the work. To get rid of this desperate mood I wrote the book 'Opera and Drama.' Last spring your article on 'Lohengrin' inspired me to such a degree that for your sake I resumed the execution of a drama quickly and joyously : this I wrote to you at the time ; but 'Siegfried's Death,' that, I knew for certain, was in the first instance impossible. I found that I should have to prepare it by another drama, and therefore took up the long cherished idea of making the 'Young Siegfried' the subject of a poem. In it everything that in 'Siegfried's Death' was either narrated or more or less taken for granted was to be shown in bold and vivid outline by means of actual representation.

" This poem was soon sketched and completed. When I was going to send it to you, I for the first time felt a peculiar anxiety. It seemed as if I could not possibly send it to you without explanation, as if I had many things to tell you, partly as to the manner of representation and partly as to the necessary comprehension of the poem itself. In the first instance it occurred to me that I still had many and various things to communicate previous to my coming before my friends with this poem. It was for that reason that I wrote the long preface to my three earlier operatic poems, of which mention has already been made.

After this I was going to begin the composition, and found, to my joy, that the music adapted itself to these verses quite naturally and easily, as if of its own accord. But the very commencement of the work reminded me that I should ruin my health entirely if I did not take care of it thoroughly before yielding to my impulse and finishing the work at a stretch and probably without interruption. When I went to the hydropathic establishment I felt compelled at last to send you the poem, but, strangely enough, something always seemed to restrain me. I was led to hesitate, because I felt as if your acquaintance with this poem would place you in a certain awkward position, as if you would not exactly know what to make of it, whether to receive it with hope or diffidence. At last, on mature consideration, my plan in its logical sequence became clear to me. Listen to me:

"This 'Young Siegfried' also is no more than a fragment, and as a separate entity it cannot produce its proper and sure impression until it occupies its necessary place in a complete whole, a place which I now assign to it, together with 'Siegfried's Death,' in my newly designed plan. In these two dramas a number of necessary relations were left to the narrative or even to the sagacity of the hearer. Everything that gave to the action and the character of these two dramas their infinitely touching and widely spreading significance had to be omitted in the representation, and could be communicated to the mind alone. But, according to my inmost conviction since formed, a work of art, and especially a drama, can have its true effect only when the poetic intention in all its more important motives speaks fully to the senses, and I cannot and dare not sin against this truth which I have recognized. I am compelled, therefore, to communicate my entire myth in its deepest and widest significance with the greatest artistic precision, so as to be fully understood. Nothing in it must in any sense be left to be supplied by thought or reflection; the unsophisticated human mind must be enabled by its artistic receptivity to comprehend the whole, because by that means only may the most detached parts be rightly understood.

"Two principal motives of my myth therefore remain to be represented, both of which are hinted at in 'Young Siegfried,' the first in the long narrative of *Brünhilde* after her awakening (Act III.), the second in the scene between *Alberich* and the *Wanderer* in the second act, and between the *Wanderer* and *Mime* in the first. That to this I was led not only by artistic reflection, but by the splendid and—for the purpose of representation—extremely rich material of these motives, you will readily under-stand when you consider the subject more closely. Think, then, of the wondrously fatal love of *Siegmund* and *Sieglinde*, of *Wotan* in his deep, mysterious relation to that love, in his dispute with *Fricka*, in his terrible self-contention when, for the sake of custom, he decrees the death of *Siegmund*, finally of the glorious Valkyr *Brünhilde* as, divining the innermost thought of *Wotan*, she disobeys the god and is punished by him; consider this wealth of motive indicated in the scene between the *Wanderer* and the *Wala*, and at greater length in the above mentioned tale of *Brünhilde*, as the material of a drama which precedes the two 'Siegfrieds,' and you will understand that it was not a reflection but rather enthusiasm which inspired my latest plan.

"That plan extends to three dramas : (1) 'The Valkyr ;' (2) 'Young Siegfried ;' (3) 'Siegfried's Death.' In order to give everything completely these three dramas must be preceded by a grand introductory play, 'The Rape of the Rhinegold.' The object is the complete representation of everything in regard to this rape—the origin of the Nibelung treasure, the possession of that treasure by *Wotan* and the curse of *Alberich*, which in 'Young Siegfried' occur in the form of a narrative. By the distinctness of representation which is thus made possible, and which at the same time does away with everything of the nature of a lengthy narrative, or at least condenses it in a few pregnant moments, I gain sufficient space to intensify the wealth of relations, while in the previous semi-tropical mode of treatment I was compelled to cut down and very much enfeeble all this.

" The entire cycle of dramas must be represented in rapid sequence, and their external embodiment can be thought of only in the following favorable circumstances : The performance of my 'Nibelung' dramas will have to take place at a great festival, to be arranged perhaps especially for the purpose of this performance. It will have to extend over three consecutive days, the introductory drama to be given on the previous evening.

" Where and in what circumstances such a performance may become possible I must not for the present consider, for first of all I have to complete my great work, and that will take me at least three years if I have any regard for my health.'

The " Ring of the Nibelung" dramas were privately printed in 1853. At least one of them, "Siegfried's Death," underwent not long afterward a change of title to " The Dusk of the Gods," and was treated to an infusion of metaphysics of the Schopenhauer school, which affected also " Young Siegfried" (now " Siegfried") by percolation. The details of these metaphysical changes are described in a thoughtful essay, "Some of Wagner's Heroes and Heroines," by William F. Apthorp, in *Scribner's Magazine,* to which those who are especially interested in this phase of the Wagnerian drama are referred. An investigation of the system of a German metaphysician and its effect upon another person who, besides being a German, is a composer with a strong tendency toward metaphysics, is rather a thankless task, and for the purpose of this biography it is sufficient, as far as the " Ring of the Nibelung" is concerned, to state that its metaphysical significance is explained in the analysis which forms part of Vol. II. of this work.

The letter to Liszt in which Wagner describes the influence of Schopenhauer upon him seems to have been written in the latter part of 1854. In the correspondence it is given without date. Wagner writes :

" I have of late occupied myself exclusively with a man who has come like a gift from heaven, although only a literary one, into my solitude. This is Arthur Schopenhauer, the greatest philosopher since Kant ; whose thoughts, as he himself expresses it, he has thought out to the end. The German professors ignored him very prudently for forty years ; but recently, to the disgrace of Germany, he has been discovered by an English critic. All the Hegels, &c., are charlatans by the side of him. His chief idea, the final negation of the desire of life, is terribly serious, but it shows the only salvation possible. To me, of course, that thought was not new, and it can indeed be conceived by no one in whom it did not pre-exist ; but this philosopher was the first to place it clearly before me. If I think of the storm of my heart, the terrible tenacity with which, against my desire, it used to cling to the hope of life, and if even now I feel this hurricane within me, I have at least found a quietus which in wakeful nights helps me to sleep. This is the genuine, ardent longing for death, for absolute unconsciousness, total non-existence ; freedom from all dreams is our only final salvation."

Wagner's work on his " Nibelung " was occasionally interrupted by other duties. In May, 1852, he superintended the production of " The Flying Dutchman " at Zurich. Writing to Liszt of the performance he says :

" ' The Flying Dutchman ' has made an indescrib-

able impression here. Philistines who never **go** to
a theatre or concert attended each of the four performances in one week and are supposed to have gone
mad. With the women I have made a great hit.
The piano scores sell by the half dozen. I am
now in the country and feel tolerably cheerful. My
work also pleases me again. My ‘ Nibelung’ tetralogy
is completely designed, and in a few months the verse
also will be finished. After that I shall be wholly and
entirely a ‘music maker,’ for this work will be my last
poem and a littérateur I hope I shall never be again.
Then I shall have nothing but plans for performances
in my head ; no more writing, only performing. I
hope you will help me.” Fortunately Wagner’s own
prognostication of his career was erroneous, otherwise we should not have had “ Tristan,” “ Meistersinger ” and “ Parsifal.” The production of “ The Flying Dutchman,” as may be judged from the above,
acted as an artistic incentive upon him and raised his
spirits. In the same letter he adds humorously :

“ I am sorry to think that you will not be able to
manage ‘Lohengrin ’ for such a long time ; the pause
is too long. As a punishment I shall dedicate the
score to you when it appears in print. I do not ask
you whether you will accept the dedication or not, for
punishment there must be.”

But “ The Flying Dutchman ” satisfied only temporarily the longing to hear his own music that was
gnawing at his heart. To look at his scores did not
stimulate him. It was like contemplating the face of
a beautiful woman who was dumb, yet whose voice

he was longing to have fall upon his ears. This grief often found expression in his letters to Liszt. Thus, referring to the production of " Lohengrin " at Weimar, he writes to Liszt :

" I control myself violently, and let no one see it ; but to you I must confess my sorrow is great not to hear my work under your direction. But I have to bear so many things I shall bear this also." And not long after the production of " The Flying Dutchman " at Zurich he was again in a wretchedly unhappy state. " I am going from bad to worse every day," he writes to Liszt, " and lead an indescribably worthless life. Of real enjoyment of life I know nothing ; to me ' enjoyment of life, of love,' is a matter of imagination, not of experience. In this manner my heart has to go to my brain, and my life becomes an artificial one; only as an ' artist ' I can live ; in the artist my whole ' man ' has been sunk. If I could visit you in Weimar, and see a performance of my operas now and then, I might perhaps still hope to recover. I should there find an element of excitement, of attraction for my artistic being ; perhaps a word of love would meet me now and then—but here ! Here I must perish in the very shortest space of time, and everything — everything will come too late, too late ! So it will be."

At times he was so cast down that he turned even from his " Nibelung " dramas : " What fate this poem —the poem of my life and of all that I am and feel— will have I cannot as yet determine. So much, however, is certain : that if Germany is not very soon open to me, and if I am compelled to drag on my artistic existence without nourishment and attraction, my animal instinct of life will soon lead me to abandon art altogether. What I shall do then to support my life I do not know, but I shall not write the music of the 'Nibelungen,' and no person with human feelings can ask me to remain the slave of my art any longer." He had hoped that "Tannhäuser" would be given in Berlin early in 1853, but it had to give way to Flotow's "Indra." Smarting under this disappointment he writes:

"I must hear 'Lohengrin;' I will not and cannot write music before." And, "For me there is no salvation but death. Would that it found me in a storm at sea, not in a sick bed. Yea, in the fire of Valhall I should like to perish. Consider well my new poem; it contains the beginning and the end of the world."

In order to satisfy his longing to hear parts of his latest work he arranged a concert at Zurich in 1853, placing a number of pieces from "Lohengrin" on the program. "I undertake the whole thing," he writes, "only to hear something out of 'Lohengrin,' and would willingly abandon the substitute if I could once hear the real 'Lohengrin.'" The work and excitement of preparation and the interest in his art which they reawakened in him greatly raised his spirits and his letters reflect his temporary cheerfulness. Referring to a remittance from Liszt he writes jocosely:

"To my disgrace I must confess that it came very conveniently, although it curiously reminded me of the fact that last year I visited the islands of Lago Maggiore at the expense of friend Liszt. Lord knows, I shall always remain a disreputable fellow. Why do you have anything to do with me ? "

His good spirits are also reflected in the following extracts from the correspondence : "On May 22 I shall be forty. Then I shall have myself rebaptized ; would you not like to be my godfather ? I wish we two could start straight from here to go into the wide world. * * * When once I have cast everything aside to dive up to the ears into the fount of music, it will sound so well that people shall hear what they cannot see."

What he wrote of the concert . itself is interesting, especially as recording his own impression of "Lohengrin." " Everything went off right well, and Zurich was astonished that such a thing could have happened. The Philistines almost carry me on their hands, and if I cared for external success the effect of my performance would more than satisfy me. But, as you know, my chief object was to hear something of ' Lohengrin,' and especially the orchestral prelude, which interested me uncommonly. The impression was most powerful, and I had to make every effort not to break down. So much is certain ; I shall fully share your predilection for 'Lohengrin;' it is the best thing I have done so far. On the public also it had the same effect. In spite of the ' Tannhäuser' overture preceding them, the pieces from 'Lohengrin' made such an impression that they were unanimously declared to be the best thing." Certainly Wagner had in himself a disciple.

critic and reporter of whose lack of interest he could hardly complain.

In giving a description of the rehearsals he speaks of studying his choruses with amateurs, and says that "these tame, four part people at last sang as if they had swallowed the devil." But the stimulating effect of this musical activity was of short duration. "'The Rhinegold' is done," he writes, "but I also am done. * * * I have no faith, and only one hope ; sleep, sleep so profound, so profound that all sensation of the pain of living ceases. * * * While here I chew a beggar's crust. I hear from Boston that 'Wagner nights' are given there. * * * Something must be done in London ; I will even go to America to satisfy my future creditor ; this, too, I offer, so that I may finish the music of my 'Nibelung' dramas." * * *

"Dearest Franz, none of my latter years has passed without bringing me at least once to the verge of the resolution to put an end to my life. Everything seems so waste, so lost ! Dearest friend, art with me, after all, is a pure stop gap, nothing else, a stop gap in the literal sense of the word. I have to stop the gap by its means in order to live at all. It is there-fore with genuine despair that I always resume art ; if I am to do this, if I am to dive into the waves of artistic fancy in order to find contentment in a world of imagination, my fancy should at least be buoyed up, my imagination supported. I cannot live like a dog ; I cannot sleep on straw and drink bad whiskey. I must be coaxed in one way or another if my mind is to accomplish the terribly difficult task of creating a non-existing world.

"Well, when I resumed the plan of the 'Nibelungen' and its actual execution, many things had to co-operate in order to produce in me the necessary, luxurious art mood. I had to adopt a better style of life than before; the success of 'Tannhäuser,' which I had surrendered solely in this hope, was to assist me. I made my domestic arrangements on a new scale. I wasted (Good Lord, wasted!) money on one or the other requirement of luxury. Your visit in the summer, for example, everything, tempted me to a forcibly cheerful deception, or rather desire of deception, as to my circumstances. My income seemed to me an infallible thing. But after my return from Paris my situation again became precarious; the expected orders for my operas, and especially for 'Lohengrin,' did not come in; and as the year approaches its close I realize that I shall want much, very much, money in order to live in my nest a little longer. * * *

"This work is truly the only thing which still ties me to the desire of life. When I think of sacrifices and demand sacrifices, it is for this work; in it alone I discover an object of my life. For its sake I must hold out, and hold out here, where I have got a foothold and have settled down to work. * * * I have in my head 'Tristan and Isolde,' the simplest but most full blooded musical conception; with the 'black flag' which floats at the end of it I shall cover myself to die. * * * *Brünnhilde* sleeps; I am, alas, still awake. * * * 'Tannhauser' and 'Lohengrin' I have thrown to the winds. I do not want to know any more of them. When I gave them over to theatrical jobbery I cast them out, I condemned them to the task of begging for me, of getting me money, *nothing but money.*"

About the only gleam of good spirits in the correspondence about this time is the following: "Do not look out for a copyist. Madame Wesendonck has given me a gold pen of indestructible power which has once more turned me into a ·calligraphic pedant. The scores will be my most perfect masterpiece of calligraphy. One cannot fly from his destiny. Meyerbeer, years ago, admired nothing so much in my scores as the neat writing. This act of admiration has been my curse; I must write neat scores as long as I live in this world."

In February, 1855, "Tannhäuser" was given in Zurich under Von Bulow's direction. A little before this production Wagner had fully remodeled his "Faust" overture. Several interesting passages in the correspondence relate to this work. Late in January, 1848, Wagner sent the score in its original form to Liszt, writing at the same time:

"As I know of no reason to withhold it from you, except that it does not please me any longer, I send it to you, because I think that in this matter the only important question is whether the overture pleases you. If the latter should be the case dispose of my work; only I should like occasionally to have the manuscript back again."

Later on he explains to Liszt—who had commented on the absence of any theme typical of *Gretchen* in the work—that his intention had been to write an entire "Faust" symphony, and adds : .

" The first movement, that which is ready, was this 'solitary Faust,' longing, despairing, cursing. The 'feminine' floats around him as an object of his longing, but not in its divine reality, and it is just this insufficient image of his longing which he destroys in his despair. The second movement was to introduce *Gretchen*, the woman. I had a theme for her, but it was only a theme. The whole remained unfinished. I wrote my 'Flying Dutchman' instead. This is the whole explanation. If now, for a last remnant of weakness and vanity, I hesitate to abandon this 'Faust' work altogether, I shall certainly have to remodel it, but only as regards instrumental modulation. The theme which you desire I cannot introduce ; this would naturally involve an entirely new composition, for which I have no inclination. If I publish it I shall give it its proper title, 'Faust in Solitude' or 'The Solitary Faust,' a tone poem for orchestra. * * * I cannot be angry with this composition, although many detached things in it would not now flow from my pen, especially the somewhat too plentiful brass is no longer in my mind."

In January, 1855, he announced to Liszt that he had remodeled the overture.

"It is an absurd coincident that just at this time I have been taken with a desire to remodel my old 'Faust' overture. I have made an entirely new score, have rewritten the instrumentation throughout, have made many changes, and have given more expansion and importance to the middle portion (second motive). I shall give it in a few days at a concert here, under the title of 'A Faust Overture.'"

Not long afterward Wagner forwarded the remodeled overture to Liszt, with this interesting communication :

"Herewith, dearest Franz, you receive my remodeled 'Faust' overture, which will appear very insignificant to you by the side of your 'Faust' symphony. To me the composition is interesting only on account of the time from which it dates ; this reconstruction has again endeared it to me, and with regard to the latter, I am childish enough to ask you to compare it very carefully with the first version, because I should like you to take cognizance of the effect of my experience, and of the more refined feeling I have gained. In my opinion new versions of this kind show most distinctly the spirit in which one has learned to work and the coarseness which one has cast off. You will be better pleased with the middle part. I was of course unable to introduce a new motive, because that would have involved a remodeling of almost the whole work ; all I was able to do was to develop the sentiment a little more broadly, in the form of a kind of enlarged cadence. *Gretchen*, of course, could not be introduced, only *Faust* himself."

His distressing financial burdens were somewhat lightened by an engagement to conduct the concerts of the London Philharmonic Society. Of his experi-

ence in this position he says : "A magnificent orchestra as far as the principal members go. Superb tone
—the leaders had the finest instruments I ever heard
—a strong *esprit de corps*, but no distinct style. The
fact is the Philharmonic people, orchestra and audience, consumed more music than they could possibly
digest. As a rule an hour's music takes several
hours' rehearsal; how can any conductor with a few
morning hours at his disposal be supposed to do justice to monster programs such as the directors put
before me? Two symphonies, two overtures, a con-
certo, and two or three vocal pieces at each concert!
The directors continually referred me to what they
chose to call the Mendelssohn traditions. But I suspect Mendelssohn had simply acquiesced in the traditional ways of the society. One morning when we
began to rehearse the 'Leonora' overture I was surprised; everybody appeared dull, slovenly, inaccurate,
as though the players were weary and had not slept
for a week. Was this to be tolerated from the famous Philharmonic orchestra? I stopped and addressed them in French, saying I knew what they
could do and I expected them to do it. Some understood and translated ; they were taken aback, but
they knew I was right and took it good humoredly.
We began again and the rehearsal passed off well. I
have every reason to believe the majority of the
artists really got to like me before I left London."

Among the compositions which he played in London were the overture of "Tannhäuser" and selec-
tions from "Lohengrin." He lived at 31 Milton street,

Dorset square, and afterward at 22 Portland terrace, Regent's Park, and at the latter place he completed the greater part of the instrumentation of the " Valkyr."

These two passages in letters dated from London speak for themselves : " Curious to me was the confession of some Mendelssohnians—that they had never heard and understood the overture to the ' Hebrides ' as well as under my direction."

"Quite recently a Mr. Ellerton, a rich amateur, approached me very cordially. He has heard my operas in Germany, and my portrait has been hanging in his room for two years. He is the first Englishman I have seen who does not care particularly for Mendelssohn. A fine, amiable mind." Wagner's surroundings were, however, uncongenial, and he found in his work but little stimulus to push forward the composition of his "Nibelung" dramas, or to inspire him with any hope of producing them when completed. "What I am creating at present," he writes, "shall never see the light except in perfectly congenial surroundings ; on this I will in future concentrate all my strength, my pride, and my resignation. If I die before having produced these works I shall leave them to you, and if you die without having been able to produce them in a dignified manner, you must burn them ; let that be settled."

Soon after Wagner's return to Zurich the question of trying his fortunes in America was agitated. The prospect seems, however, to have rather alarmed him, and drew from him one of the most characteristic letters in the correspondence. "America is a terrible

nightmare.   If the New York people should ever
make up their minds to offer me a considerable sum,
I should be in the most awful dilemma.   If I refused
I should have to conceal it from all men, for everyone would charge me in my position with reckless-
ness.   Ten years ago I might have undertaken such a
thing, but to have to walk in such byways now in
order to live would be too hard—now, when I am fit
only to do, and devote myself to, that which is strictly
my business.   I should never finish the 'Nibelungen'
in my life !   Good gracious ! such sums as I might
earn in America people ought to give me, without
asking anything in return beyond what I am actually
doing and which is the best that I can do.   Besides
this, I am much better adapted to spend 60,000 frs.
in six months than to 'earn' it.   The latter I cannot
do at all, for it is not my business to 'earn money,'
but it is the business of my admirers to give me as
much money as I want, to do my work in a cheerful
mood.   Well, it is a good thing, and I will take courage from the thought that the Americans will make
me no such offer."

Wagner's financial views, while interesting, would
hardly strike a business man as sound.   It may be
true in the abstract that the world owes a livelihood
to genius, but as genius is rarely recognized until after
its possessor's success or death, the income derived
from a genius fund would probably not begin until it
was too late to be of service.   Moreover, if an attempt
were made to raise a genius fund the rich men applied
to might reply—and not without some show of truth—

that it takes as much genius to make a million as it does to make music. Wagner carried his financial theory into various details of life. Thus we find him asking Liszt to apply it in the acquisition of a piano. "You must get me an Erard grand," he writes to Liszt. "Write to the widow and tell her that you visit me three times every year, and that you must absolutely have a better grand piano than the old and lame one in my possession. Tell her a hundred thousand fibs, and make her believe that it is for her a point of honor that an Erard should stand in my house. In brief, do not think but act with the impudence of genius. I must have an Erard. If they will not give me one let them lend me one on a yard long lease."

This was written in July, 1856. A pleasant incident of his life during the same year was a visit from Liszt at St. Gallen, in November, when Wagner conducted the "Eroica" and Liszt his "Orpheus" and "Preludes."

As far as the various interruptions to which he was subjected would allow he had, since he had finished the "Nibelung" dramas in 1853, been at work on the music of these. He says himself, in a letter to the Italian composer Arrigo do Boïto, that the music of the "Rhinegold" occurred to him during a sleepless night at an inn in Spezzia, and that he straightway turned homeward and set to work on the score. By May, 1854, the music of the "Rhinegold" was finished. The following month he began the "Valkyr" and finished all but the instrumentation during the following winter and the full score in 1856. Previous to this, in fact already in the autumn of 1854, he had sketched some of the music of " Siegfried," and in the spring of 1857 the full score of the first act and of the greater part of the second act was finished.

Besides the various extracts from the correspondence relating to this work already given there are others equally interesting. Thus he wrote early in 1855 : " The score of the first act of the ' Valkyr ' will soon be ready ; it is wonderfully beautiful. I have done nothing like it or approaching it before ;" and in October of the same year : " At times, when I was timid and sobered down, I was chiefly anxious about the great scene of *Wotan*, especially when he discloses the decrees of fate to *Brünnhilde*, and in London I was once on the point of rejecting the whole scene. In order to come to a decision I took up the sketch and recited the scene with proper expression, when fortunately I discovered that my spleen was unjustified, and that if properly represented the scene would have a grand effect even in a purely musical sense."

Ill health also interrupted his work. " My health, too," he writes in January, 1857, " is once more so bad that for ten days after I had finished the sketch for the first act of ' Siegfried ' I was literally not able to write a single bar without being driven away from my work by a most alarming headache. Every morning I sit down, stare at the paper, and am glad enough when I get as far as reading Walter Scott. The fact is I have once more overtaxed myself, and how am I to recover my strength ? With ' Rhine-

gold ' I got on well enough, considering my circumstances, but the 'Valkyr' caused me much pain.
At present my nervous system resembles a pianoforte very much out of tune, and on that instrument
I am expected to produce 'Siegfried.' Well, I fancy
the strings will break at last, and then there will be
an end. We cannot alter it ; this is a life fit for a
dog."

By May of the same year, however, more agreeable
surroundings had given renewed impetus to his artistic nature. "Very soon," he writes, "I hope to resume my long interrupted work, and I shall certainly
not leave my charming refuge even for the shortest
trip before *Siegfried* has settled everything with
Brünnhilde. So far I have only finished the first act,
but then it is quite ready, and has turned out stronger
and more beautiful than anything. I am astonished
myself at having achieved this, for at our last meeting I again appeared to myself a terribly blundering
musician. Gradually, however, I gained self confidence. With a local prima donna, whom you heard
in 'La Juive,' I studied the great final scene of the
'Valkyr.' Kirchner accompanied ; I hit the notes
famously, and this scene, which gave you so much
trouble, realized all my expectations. We performed
it three times at my house, and now I am quite satisfied. The fact is that everything in this scene is so
subtle, so deep, so subdued, that the most intellec-
tual, the most tender, the most perfect execution in
every direction is necessary to make it understood.
If this, however, is achieved the impression is be-

yond a doubt.   But of course a thing of this kind is
always on the verge of being quite misunderstood,
unless all concerned approach it in the most perfect,
most elevated, most intelligent mood ; merely to play
it through as we tried, in a hurried way, is impossible.   I, at least, lose on such occasions instinctively
all power and intelligence ; I become perfectly stupid.
But now I am quite satisfied, and if you hear the
melting and hammering songs of ' Siegfried ' you will
have a new experience of me.   The abominable part
of it is that I cannot have a thing of this kind played
for my own benefit.''

But *Siegfried* and *Brünnhilde* were not to settle matters between them for a number of years to come.
From a passage in the correspondence we have
already learned that in 1854 he had become acquainted with the '' Tristan '' legend.   Recognizing the difficulties which he would encounter in securing a performance of the '' Nibelung '' and, appalled by the
prospect of the battle he would be obliged to wage,
he had at times been on the verge of suspending
work on the music of the dramas and taking up
'' Tristan '' as a more practicable subject.   Thus he
wrote in 1856 : '' My only way would be to give up
the ' Nibelungen ' and begin such a simple work as
' Tristan ' instead, which would have the advantage
that I could presumably dispose of it to the theatres
at once and receive royalties in return, although, as
you know, the music trade would give me nothing
for it.''

In 1857 he was so disheartened that he abandoned

the composition of "Siegfried" at the *Waldweben* scene and turned to "Tristan." His idea was that the "Tristan" work would be short and comparatively easy to perform. Genius that he was he had an idea that because it was easy for him to write great music it would be easy for others to interpret it. A very curious, not to say laughable, incident occurred at this time. An agent of the Emperor of Brazil called and asked if Wagner would compose an opera for an Italian troupe at Rio de Janeiro, and would he conduct the work himself, all upon his own terms. Thus "Tristan" was actually composed, or, at least, the composition of it was begun, with a view of its being performed by Italians in Brazil. What a polyglot affair it would have been ! An opera on an Irish subject, composed by a German in Switzerland and sung by Italians in Brazil ! It is proper to state, however, that the Emperor of Brazil was really interested in Wagner. He subsequently became a patron of the theatre at Bayreuth and witnessed a performance of the "Ring" there.

The following, written in May, 1875, refers to his abandonment of the "Nibelung" dramas for "Tristan," and also to the latter's possible production in Rio : "For so much I may assume that a thoroughly practicable work, such as 'Tristan' is to be, will quickly bring me a good income and keep me afloat for a time. In addition to this I have a curious idea. I am thinking of having a good Italian translation made of this work in order to produce it as an Italian opera at the theatre of Rio Janeiro, which will proba-

bly give my 'Tannhäuser' first. I mean to dedicate
it to the Emperor of Brazil, who will soon receive
copies of my last three operas, and all this will, I
trust, realize enough to keep me out of harm's way
for a time. Whether after that my 'Nibelungen'
will appeal to me again I cannot foresee ; it depends
upon moods over which I have no control. For once
I have used violence against myself. Just as I was
in the most favorable mood I have torn *Siegfried*
from my heart and placed him under lock and key as
one buried alive. There I shall keep him, and no one
shall see anything of him, as I had to shut him out
from myself. Well, perhaps this sleep will do him
good ; as to his awaking I decide nothing. I had to
fight a hard and painful battle before I got to this
point. Well, it is settled so far."

The poem of "Tristan" was finished early in 1857,
and in the winter of the same year the full score
of the first act was ready to be forwarded to the
engraver, Wagner having hurried the work, as the
Härtels had promised him one-half of the honorarium
of 200 louis d'or on receipt of the first act. The
second act is dated Venice, March 2, 1859, Wagner
temporarily residing there with the permission of the
Austrian authorities. The third is dated Lyons,
August, 1859.

It is interesting to note in connection with "Tristan" that, while Wagner wrote it because he thought
it would be easy to secure its performance, he subsequently found more difficulty in getting it produced
than any other of his works. In fact, he could not

even obtain permission to return to Germany — though whether the Germans were more afraid of Wagner or of " Tristan " we have no means of knowing.

In the summer of 1858 he received a visit from Tausig and gives Liszt a graphic pen picture of this phenomenal young musician's doings :

"When he came into my room, one fine morning, bringing your letter, I shook you cordially by the hand. He is a terrible youth. I am astonished, alternately, by his highly developed intellect and his wild ways. He will become something extraordinary, if he becomes anything at all. When I see him smoking frightfully strong cigars, and drinking no end of tea, while as yet there is not the slighest hope of a beard, I am frightened, like the hen when she sees the young ducklings, which she has hatched by mistake, take to the water. What will become of him I cannot foresee, but whiskey and rum he will not get from me. I should, without hesitation, have taken him into my house, if we had not mutually molested each other by pianoforte playing. So I have found him a room in a little hole close to me, where he is to sleep and work, doing his other daily business at my house. He does, however, no credit to my table, which, in spite of my grass-widowerhood, is fairly well provided. He sits down to table every day stating that he has no appetite at all, which pleases me all the less, because the reason is the cheese and the sweets he has eaten. In this manner he tortures me continually, and devours my biscuits, which my wife doles out grudgingly even to me. He hates walking, and yet declares that he would like to come with me when I propose to leave him at home. After the first half hour he lags behind, as if he had walked four hours.

"My childless marriage is thus suddenly blessed with an interesting phenomenon, and I take in, in rapid doses, the quintessence of paternal cares and troubles. All this has done me a great deal of good ; it was a splendid diversion, for which, as I said before, I have to thank you. You knew what I wanted. Of course the youth pleases me immensely in other ways, and, although he acts like a naughty boy, he talks like an old man of pronounced character. Whatever subject I broach with him he is sure to follow me with clearness of mind and remarkable receptivity. At the same time it touches and moves me when this boy shows such deep, tender feeling, such large sympathy, that he captivates me irresistibly. As a musician he is enormously gifted, and his furious piano playing makes me tremble. I must always think of you and of the strange influence which you exercise over so many, and often considerably gifted, young men. I cannot but call you happy and genuinely admire your harmonious being and existence."

In September, 1859, he again went to Paris with the somewhat curious hope that he could there find opportunity to produce " Tristan " with German artists, or at least obtain a French performance of " Tannhäuser " or "Lohengrin." Regarding " Tristan," he writes from Paris to Liszt : " The first act of ' Tristan, which I have brought with me, has aroused me wonderfully. It is a remarkable piece of music. I feel a strong desire to communicate some of it to someone, and I fear I shall be tempted to play some of it to Berlioz one of these days, although my beautiful performance will probably terrify and disgust him. Could I only be with you! That, you know, is the burden of my song." There is an amusing description of a reading of "Lohengrin" for the benefit of Carvalho, director of the Lyric Theatre, with Wagner at the piano. He is described as sitting at the instrument struggling with the finale of the second act, singing, yelling and gesticulating as if demented. Carvalho is represented as going through the ordeal quietly and patiently, and finally bringing the matter to a close with a few polite words. Early in 1860 Wagner gave in Paris three orchestral and choral concerts, which added not a little to his fame and to his debts, and he was obliged to part with a portion of the sum paid by the Schotts for the copyright of the "Ring." Nothing daunted, however, he gave, with similar results, two concerts at the Brussels Opera House. But now a new hope was held out to him. Through the intercession of the Princess Metternich, the Emperor ordered the production of "Tannhäuser" at the Opéra, commanding that the work should be mounted in the most magnificent style, and that Wagner should choose his own singers and have as many rehearsals as he saw fit. Chief among the singers whom he selected was Niemann, for the title rôle.

There were seventy-three rehearsals at the piano forty-five choral, twenty-seven without orchestra on the stage, four for scenic changes, and fourteen full rehearsals with orchestra—a hundred and fifty-three in all. The production is said to have cost something like $40,000. He rewrote the opening scene entirely, and, as a sort of a preliminary educational campaign, published a translation of several of his librettos, with a prefatory explanation of his aims and views. Nevertheless he was not sanguine of success. The conductor of the Opéra, whose place Wagner was anxious to fill himself for this occasion, was Dietsche, none other than the man who had set the French version of "The Flying Dutchman" to music. It is easy to understand that he could not have been very kindly disposed toward the author and musician who had produced a successful opera on the same subject, and he probably thought this was a good chance to compass the shipwreck of a person whom he could regard as little more than the *Flying Dutchman* among composers. Nevertheless, the opera probably would have achieved success, had it not been for the opposition of the famous Jockey Club, among them many of the old nobility who had come to look upon the opera as nothing else than a pleasing frame for a grand ballet, so timed that it would begin just about as they came to the opera from their club dinner.

The manager of the Opéra made every effort to induce Wagner to introduce a ballet into the second act of "Tannhäuser," but Wagner's artistic conscience was not elastic. As a result, the members of the

Jockey Club were determined from the start that the opera should be doomed to failure. In this way they could show not only their displeasure at the omission of the ballet, but also, at the same time, disrespect toward the Emperor, whom they regarded as little more than an upstart. As a failure this performance was probably the greatest success on record. It is actually historical. Nothing that Wagner did could be otherwise than grand, and therefore the failure was on an enormous scale. Three performances were given, of which it is difficult to say whether the performance was on the stage or in the auditorium, for the uproar in the house certainly drowned whatever sounds came from the stage. The members of the Jockey Club and their hirelings armed themselves with shrill whistles, on which they began to blow whenever there was the slightest hint of applause, and the result was that between the efforts of the singers to make themselves heard and of Wagner's friends to applaud, and the shrill whistling from his enemies, there was confusion worse confounded. But Wagner's friendship with Princess Metternich bore good fruit. Through her mediation, it is supposed, he received permission to return to all parts of Germany but Saxony. It was not until March, 1862, thirteen years later, that he was again allowed to enter the kingdom of his birth and first success.

In another way, too, the Paris failure bore good results. It produced a certain loyalty to him in Germany, and when he returned there in 1861 he was received with enthusiasm. His first thought was to secure the production of "Tristan," but at Vienna, after fifty-seven rehearsals, it was put on the shelf, and negotiations with other theatres proving fruitless he was obliged to earn a precarious living by giving concerts. Those of his operas which were performed did not yield him sufficient to live on. He tells the story in his own words : " My operas were to be heard right and left; but I could not live on the proceeds. At Dresden 'Tannhäuser' and 'The Flying Dutchman' had grown into favor ; yet I was told that I had no claim with regard to them, since they were produced during my Capellmeistership, and a Hofcapellmeister in Saxony is bound to furnish an opera once a year. When the Dresden people wanted 'Tristan' I refused to let them have it unless they agreed to pay for 'Tannhäuser.' Accordingly they thought they could dispense with 'Tristan.' Afterward, when the public insisted upon 'The Mastersingers,' I got the better of them."

May 15, 1861, thirteen years after it was finished and eleven years after its first performance, Wagner heard " Lohengrin " for the first time at Vienna. He was welcomed at Weimar in August by Liszt and a large circle of musicians. As a sort of reaction from his "Tristan " he now began to elaborate the sketch of " The Mastersingers," which he made in 1845, as a humorous sequence to the contest of the minstrels in "Tannhäuser." He had finished the libretto during a temporary sojourn in Paris during the winter of 1861-2. In the latter year the poem was printed for private circulation by the Schotts, of Mayence. Wagner began to compose the music while residing in Biebrich, on the Rhine, opposite Mayence. On November 1, in the same year, he produced at a benefit concert at Leipsic the overture of "The Mastersingers." Dannreuther says: "The writer, who was present, distinctly remembers the half empty room, the almost complete absence of professional musicians, the wonderful performance and the enthusiastic demand for a repetition, in which the members of the orchestra took part as much as the audience." To this we may add Wagner's own remark: "That curious concert at Leipsic was the first of a long series of such absurd undertakings to which my straitened means led me. At other towns the public at least appeared *en masse* and I could record an artistic success, but it was not until I went to Russia that the pecuniary results were worth mentioning."

In 1863, while working upon "The Mastersingers" at Penzing, near Vienna, he published his "Nibelung" dramas, expressing his hope that through the bounty of one of the German rulers the completion and performance of his "Ring of the Nibelung" would be made possible. But in the spring of 1864, worn out by his struggle with poverty and almost broken in spirit by his contest with public and critics, he actually determined to give up his public career, and eagerly grasped the opportunity to visit a private country seat in Switzerland. Just at this very moment, when despair had settled upon him, the long wished for help came. King Ludwig II. of Bavaria sent a secretary to find Wagner and bid him come to Munich

and finish his work.   Wagner was no longer in Vienna.
He had passed through Munich on his way to Zurich,
but had happened to make a detour to Stuttgart.
Hither the secretary tracked him, and in May the an-
nouncement was published that the King of Bavaria
had allowed him a pension of $500 a year from his
private purse.

After a brief visit in Switzerland, Wagner settled in
Munich in 1864, becoming a Bavarian subject.   Here
he composed the " March of Homage " (" Huldegung's
Marsch "), in honor of King Ludwig, for military
band, but published as a work for full orchestra, and
in the autumn he was officially commissioned to complete the " Ring."   The pension was increased and a
little house in the suburbs placed at his disposal.
"Tristan" was produced at Munich, June 10, 1865,
after numerous and exacting rehearsals, under Von
Bülow, and with the only tenor whom Wagner considered competent to take the leading part, Ludwig
Schnorr v. Carolsfeld, whose wife took the part of
Isolde.   The work was repeated June 13 and 19 and
July 1.   Schnorr died suddenly at Dresden of
pneumonia July 21, 1865.   During the last scene after
Tristan's death the tenor was obliged to lie on the
stage exposed to a strong draft, which is supposed
to have brought on his fatal illness.   " Tristan " was
not, in fact could not, be given again until June, 1869,
when the Vogels took the leading part.

Owing to the ill will of Franz Lachner and other
Munich pedants, but also, it is only fair to state,
to the alleged insufficiency of available funds, his

ideas for a new music school could not be carried out.

At the same time all kinds of combinations, political as well as musical, were formed against Wagner, and in December, 1865, the King requested him to promote their mutual comfort by leaving Munich for a while. Retaining the full confidence and friendship of the King, in spite of all his enemies had done to sever their relations, Wagner again turned to his favorite asylum, Switzerland. After short stays at Vevey and Geneva, he settled at Triebschen, near ' Luzerne, which may be looked upon as his residence until he removed to Bayreuth, in 1872. At Triebschen, October 20, 1857, twenty-two years after he had made the first sketches of "The Mastersingers," the work was completed, Hans Richter having arrived there in 1866 to copy the score. June 21, 1868, a model performance of the work was given at Munich under the direction of Von Bülow, Richter acting as chorus master and Wagner supervising all the details. Dannreuther speaks of this as the finest performance of any of Wagner's works ever given. While Wagner was at Triebschen he worked steadily at the unfinished portion of the "Ring," completing the instrumentation of the third act of "Siegfried" in 1869 and the introduction and first act of "The Dusk of the Gods" in June, 1870.

August 25, 1870, his first wife having died January 25, 1866, after five years' separation from him, he married the divorced wife of Von Bülow, Cosima Liszt, whose mother was the French authoress who

wrote under the name of "Daniel Sterne." In 1869
and 1870 the "Rhinegold" and the "Valkyr" were
respectively performed at the Court Theatre in
Munich. In 1869 he published his admirable essay
on orchestral leading, and in 1870 his essay on Beethoven.

Bayreuth having been determined upon as the
place where a theatre for the special production of
his "Ring" should be built, Wagner settled there in
April, 1872. On his sixtieth birthday, May 22, he
celebrated the laying of the foundation of the Wagner Theatre there with a model performance of Beethoven's ninth symphony and his own "Emperor
March."

The cost of the theatre was originally esti-
mated at 300,000 thalers, and was to be raised upon
1,000 certificates, each entitling the holder to a seat
at three performances. When a considerable number
of these had been taken up—but the scheme seemed
nevertheless to have come to a standstill—the plan of
forming Wagner societies, where subscriptions for
small amounts could be contributed, was suggested.
The idea was adopted with enthusiasm, and it may
be said that these societies sprang up nearly all over
the civilized world. . Under the auspices of a number
of these Wagner conducted concerts which helped
materially to swell the fund. By November, 1874,
"The Dusk of the Gods" received its finishing touches,
and rehearsals had already been held at Bayreuth.
During the summer of 1875, under Wagner's supervision, Hans Richter held full rehearsals there, and

there was every promise that the master's intentions would be realized.

In November and December, 1875, Wagner superintended rehearsals of "Tannhäuser" and "Lohengrin" at Vienna, which were performed, without cuts, on November 22 and December 15. "Tristan," also under his supervision, was given at Berlin on March 20, 1876.

At last, twenty-eight years after its first conception, on August 13th, 14th, 16th and 17th, again from August 20 to 23 and from August 27 to 30, 1876, "The Ring of the Nibelung" was performed at Bayreuth with the following cast: *Wotan*, Betz; *Loge*, Vogel; *Alberich*, Hill; *Mime*, Schlosser; *Fricka*, Frau Grun; *Donner* and *Gunther*, Gura; *Erda* and *Waltraute*, Frau Jaide; *Siegmund*, Niemann; *Sieglinde*, Frl. Schefsky; *Brünnhilde*, Frau Materna; *Siegfried*, Unger; *Hagen*, Siehr; *Gutrune*, Frl. Wecklerin; *Rheindaughters*, Lili and Marie Lehman and Frl. Lammert. First violin; Wilhelmj; conductor, Hans Richter. From a musical point of view the performance was correct throughout—in many instances of surpassing excellence; sundry shortcomings on the stage were owing more to want of money than to anything else. In spite of the sacrifice readily made by each and all of the artists concerned, there was a heavy deficit—about $37,500—the responsibility for which pressed upon Wagner. He had hoped to be able to repeat the performances in the following summer. This proved impossible, and his efforts to discharge the debts of the theatre failed for the most part.

The most important of these efforts, the Wagner Festival at the Albert Hall in London, 1877, nearly involved him in further difficulties. These concerts were given at the instance of Wilhelmj with an orchestra of 170 and several of the leading singers from Bayreuth, among them Materna, Hill and Unger. Wagner was able to remit about $3,500 to Bayreuth. After his return a considerable sum was forwarded to him as a testimonial, but he was able to return it with a letter of thanks, he having decided to cover the debt of the Bayreuth performances from royalties to come from performances of the "Ring" at Munich. During his third stay in London, April 30 to June 4, he lived at 12 Orme square, Bayswater. Of his conducting Dannreuther said : " Was Wagner really a great conductor? There can be no doubt that he was, particularly with regard to the works of Weber and Beethoven. His perfect sympathy with these led him to find the true tempi as it were by intuition. He was thoroughly at home in the orchestra, though he had never learned to play upon any orchestral instrument. He had an exquisite sense for beauty of tone, nuances of tempo, precision and proportion of rhythm. His beat was distinct, and his extraordinary power of communicating his enthusiasm to the executants never failed. The writer was present at one of the great occasions when he appeared as conductor—the rehearsals and performance of the ninth symphony at Bayreuth, May 22, 1872— and felt that for spirit and perfection of phrasing it was the finest musical performance within the whole range of his musical experience. But at the Albert Hall Wagner did not do himself justice. His strength was already on the wane. The rehearsals fatigued him and he was frequently faint in the evening. His memory played him tricks and his beat was nervous. Still there were moments when his great gifts appeared as of old. Those who witnessed his conducting of the ' Kaisermarsch ' at the first rehearsal he attended (May 5) will never forget the superb effect."

The poem of "Parsifal" was published in December, 1877. Wagner had taken it in manuscript to London with him, where he read it for the first time to a circle of friends. He had originally intended that the "Ring" should be performed only at Bayreuth, but for financial reasons he was obliged to allow it to make the rounds of the German theatres, which it did, and is still doing very successfully. January, 1878, the first number of the "Bayreuther Blätter," published by and for the Wagner Verein, under the editorship of Hans von Wolzogen, appeared. To this Wagner himself contributed a number of interesting papers. He was sixty-five years old when he began the music of "Parsifal," completing the sketch of the first act early in the spring of 1878, of the second October 11, beginning the third shortly after Christmas, and completing it in April, 1879. In the winter of this year he was obliged to go to Southern Italy for his health, having suffered from erysipelas. The instrumentation of "Parsifal" was finished at Palermo, January 13, 1882. The introduction had been heard privately at Bayreuth, Christmas, 1878, played by the Meiningen

Orchestra. "Parsifal" was produced in July, 1882, sixteen performances, extending into August, being given. It has been frequently repeated since then. The Bayreuth performances, since the first production of the "Ring," have been given with good profit.

In the autumn of 1882, Wagner's health being in an unsatisfactory state, though no alarming symptoms had shown themselves, he took up his residence in Venice at the Palazzo Vendramini, on the Grand Canal. He wrote for the "Bayreuther Blätter," and conducted the private performance of his symphony, already referred to. But the afternoon of February 13, 1883, he died suddenly of heart disease. He had risen at six in the morning and been busily at work, it is believed on instructions for the next summer's Bayreuth festival. For dinner he had taken at one o'clock only a plate of soup in his room. Soon afterwards the maid who was always on duty in the ante-room heard him faintly calling her. When she reached him he was prone on the floor, and could only gasp : "Call my wife and the doctor." These were his last words. The body was sent from Venice in state to Bayreuth, where it was buried in a vault built by himself in a retired corner of the garden which surrounds his house.

Wagner was under middle height, quick in movement, speech and gesture and erect of carriage ; but, after all, his physical appearance was very disappointing to anyone who knew him simply through his works. He had, however, a tremendous forehead, indicating his immense energy and will power, which, in spite of his morbid, artistic disposition, carried him triumphantly over many distressing periods of

his life. In the police circular which was issued for
his arrest by the Saxon authorities, after the political
riot of 1849, he is described as follows : " Wagner
is thirty-seven to thirty-eight years old, of middle
height, has brown hair, wears glasses, open forehead,
eyebrows brown, eyes gray blue, nose and mouth
well proportioned, chin round ; particulars, in moving and speaking he is hasty ; clothing, surtout of
dark green buckskin, trousers of black cloth, velvet
waistcoat, silk handkerchief, the usual felt hat and
boots." He seems to have been a kindly man in his
own home, especially after his union to his sympathetic and congenial second wife. One can readily
understand the irritated attitude he assumed toward
the public, critics and managers.

His great works, which are the delight of thou-
sands, had actually to fight their way, note by note,
until they were appreciated. And even now, when
his works may be said to have triumphed, dissenting
voices are heard. Yet one needs but to approach him
in a proper spirit to appreciate his works. I can remember well that at Bayreuth in 1882 the very children in the streets whistled motives from " Parsifal,"
showing that after all his music cannot be so terribly
abstruse. The fact is that Wagner is most easily approached from an entirely unbiased standpoint, and
those who have not through previous acquaintance
with the works of his predecessors dropped into a
certain groove are often those who most readily appreciate him. I once attended a concert with a companion who was but slightly acquainted with classical

works and had heard nothing of Wagner's. At this
concert there was given a symphony by Beethoven,
and among the other pieces the introduction and
finale of "Tristan." I was quite struck with the ease
with which my friend grasped Wagner's intentions. The
"Tristan" music seemed perfectly simple and intelligible to him, and it was really a treat to witness his delight on hearing it. But Beethoven puzzled him as much
as Wagner would puzzle a champion of conservative
form in music. Beethoven seemed to him con-
strained and artificial, Wagner natural and free in his
methods. I have heard of others who have had a
similar experience. Wagner in private life is described as a thorough gentleman, yet unconventional,
with an artist's fondness for artistic and even luxurious surroundings. There is authority for stating distinctly that the reports in the German newspapers regarding his lavish self indulgence were fabrications.
One of these accounts stated that he had a hundred
dressing gowns, all of rich material and of different
colors, of the most delicate variety. Wagner, on hearing this report, said, laughingly, that of these hundred dressing gowns he had all but ninety-nine.

The discourtesy, dishonesty and virulence to which
Wagner was subjected in Germany were great.
Not only his works but his private character was violently assailed. It is a great pity that he did not have
the disposition to let these things pass by unnoticed.
But it must be remembered that these attacks were
not only insults to him personally—they were actual
hindrances in his artistic and in his worldly career.

They prevented the production of his works, and thus kept him in a constant state of impoverished distress, depriving him for many years of the necessary leisure to complete the great works he had in his mind, simply because his poverty compelled him to do all kinds of musical drudgery in order to eke out a livelihood. How many more great works Wagner would have given us it is difficult to say, nor is it perhaps a very gracious task to speculate upon this matter, when we consider how rich our inheritance from him is. From " Rienzi " to " Parsifal " is a steady development. His powers were ever on the increase. The " Ring " is not, as some have said, a greater work than " Parsifal." The latter does not show any falling off in powers. If the themes heard in it are not on the same grand, titanic scale as those of the " Ring," it is because the subject called for an entirely different style of treatment.

There is nothing in " Parsifal " to show that he could not, had he but wanted to, have written another " Ring," whereas there is much in it of a different but in some respects superior kind of beauty. He has certainly in " Parsifal " succeeded in giving the most exquisite expressions to the deepest religious feeling —for *Parsifal* is really an allegorical personation of Christ—and if we consider religious feeling the most exalted of all emotions, we must agree that Wagner has in " Parsifal " struck finer chords than in any other of his works. He was a man of wide literary culture. He, as we remember, was familiar with Shakespeare from his youth. To hear him read or act a scene from Shakespeare was said to be a delight never to be forgotten, and when in particularly good spirits he would take up a comic scene and render it with the exuberant merriment of a child. Scott and Carlyle were also well represented in his library. He had Sanscrit, Greek and Roman classics, Italian writers from Dante to Leopardi, Spanish, English and French dramatists and philosophic writings from Plato to Schopenhauer. He also possessed a remarkably complete collection of French and German mediæval stories and Norse legends, together with a vast number of philological comments thereon. History and fiction were also well represented.

BAYREUTH ECHOES.

WAGNER THEATRE.

BAYREUTH ECHOES.[*]

ONE of the greatest obstacles in the way of attending a performance at Bayreuth is the difficulty of getting to Bayreuth at all. It requires considerable ingenuity, and whoever has discovered the route there may be sure that he knows more than most of the German railroad officials. Of course, I didn't expect that the sleepy Belgians in Ostend would be able to direct me, but I did think that the officials in Aix la Chapelle, or in a railroad centre like Cologne, would know the way. It was not, however, until I had reached Mainz—after traveling from 3:50 A. M. till 4:28 P. M.—that I could obtain fairly detailed directions. And yet placards announcing the "Parsifal" performances were hanging up in the depots all along the route!

I traveled on the lightning express from Cologne to Mainz. This lightning express goes at the tremendous rate of twenty miles an hour, stops only about fifteen times and then only long enough for all the

* In 1882 the author was the New York *World's* correspondent at the production of "Parsifal" at Bayreuth.

conductors—it takes half a dozen conductors to run this train—and passengers to walk leisurely to a neighboring restaurant, drink a glass of beer and get comfortably into their coupés again. So I calculated that it takes the average German five hours and fifteen refreshments to get from Cologne to Mainz. An elderly gentleman in the same coupé with me, who had heard me inquiring the way to Bayreuth at Cologne, kindly consulted his German A B C railroad guide book for about two hours, and then informed me that as far as he could make out I had better go from Mainz over Darmstadt, Aschaffenburg and Würzburg to Bamberg instead of over Frankfort. Bamberg, he said, was in the direction of Bayreuth. He then tried to find out in his German A B C guide book how to get from Bamberg to Bayreuth, but as we were only an hour and a half from Mainz he didn't have time. He also informed me that our train made very close connection at Mainz for the Darmstadt train. "But," he added, " if you want to make inquiries at the ticket office as to the best way of getting to Bayreuth simply explain matters to the Oberstationsvorsteher " (which is a German linguistic short cut for station master) "and he will hold the train for you."

Fortunately a six years' previous residence in Germany had taught me that if I called this station master by his full title and pronounced each of the eight syllables in Oberstationsvorsteher distinctly he would hold the train at least two minutes for each syllable. And sure enough he did hold the train long enough for me to make my inquiries leisurely. So, sixteen minutes behind time, the lightning express crawled out of Mainz and brought me to Bamberg at midnight. Here I had to wait until 4 A. M. for a train to Bayreuth, arriving there at 8 A. M.

The readiness of almost every foreign railroad official or servant in any capacity to prey upon strangers was strongly impressed upon me during this trip. I don't understand how a foreigner who can't speak the language gets home with any money at all in his pocket. These officials and menials will try to exchange your American or English money at exorbitant rates ; if they find you are not *au fait* in the currency of the country they will give you wrong change ; they will overcharge everything. Let a foreigner enter a hotel and the whole house, from the proprietor down to the boots, makes a dead set at him and tries to cheat him out of as much as possible. You think the Portier very polite when he bows very low to you as he hands you your letters. You think that the waiter's cordial good morning comes straight from the heart, and you are touched by the simple cordiality you see around you. But you are mistaken. The hope of a few pence will induce these people to play the hypocrite for a month. They are only acting. They smile and bow and scrape only because they hope that when you go away you will drop a *pourboire* into their hand.

When I arrived in Bayreuth I found the town in a state of confusion. One would suppose that the experience in 1872, when the foundation stone of the Wagner Theatre was laid, and in 1876, when the

"Nibelungen Ring" was produced, would have taught those worthy burghers to be prepared to accommodate strangers. But no—they had been awakened from a long sleep in 1872 and then had gone to sleep again until 1876. Then at least they might have stayed awake till 1882. But the strangers well plucked and out of the town, and the inhabitants were sound asleep again. I get to the hotel and find the proprietor cursing the Portier, the Portier cursing the head waiter, the head waiter cursing the waiter, and the waiter cursing the boots, who revenged himself by kicking a cat. Everyone about the house—except the cat—had lost his head.

I breakfasted with a Russian who had come on the same train with me. He had spent the last ten years hunting after Wagner operas. When he had heard of a Wagner opera being given somewhere he had taken the first train for that place. In this way he had managed to hear Wagner music about every other night. He had just come from the thirty Wagner performances in London and had tickets for the sixteen "Parsifal" performances. He told me very seriously that when he first saw the Alps he fell on his knees and wept; also that he had been similarly affected only once before in his lfe—as he passed the Acropolis of Athens.

The night I arrived I had the unexpected pleasure of seeing a comedy. It was a genuine German comedy, too. Its subject matter was the efforts of the Bayreuth fire brigade to put out a fire. I was awakened from a sound sleep by the loud beating of a drum under my windows. I could hear drums beating in various parts of the city, the church bells were ringing, there was the heavy tramp of soldiers through the streets, people rushing about and shouting fire—in fact, every indication of a fire, except the noise of fire engines. A house a little way down the street was burning. A crowd had gathered there. I found the infantry guarding a patch of beans, the cavalry stationed about the potato patch with flashing sabres, and the artillery drawn up around a pear tree. The flames were crackling merrily among the beams. The house might burn down, but the warriors of the Vaterland were prepared to defend those beans, those potatoes and that pear tree with the last drop of their blood. At last, around the corner appeared six big firemen carrying a small ladder, and after them six small firemen carry a big ladder. They wore green suits and brass helmets. When they had managed to place the big ladder against the front of the house they ran away again.

After a while we heard a rattling as though a dog with a tin can tied to his tail were running through the next street. The twelve firemen again turned the corner, drawing after them what looked like a tin box on wheels. It was the fire engine—an open tin box with a hand pump. A hose was attached. A fireman mounted the ladder. Another fireman carried the hose up to him. Meanwhile women with large wooden panniers strapped to their backs brought water from the neighboring fountain and emptied it into the engine. Finally everything was ready and the pumping began. Several large streams of water came from holes in the hose and wet the bystanders. A small stream came from the nozzle. The fire was such a trifle that they really managed to get it pretty well under control. The next day the City Council voted a resolution of thanks and a compensation of 12½ cents to each of the women who carried the water from the fountain to the engine. During the "Parsifal" performances the firemen were distributed through the theatre. This seemed to me unnecessary—the building could have burned down without their assistance.

Bayreuth is a picturesque old town, containing a number of fine old buildings, relics of bygone days, when the Margraves housed there in splendor, the old theatre with its gorgeous Rococo decorations, and the palace from whose frieze the carved heads of the old rulers gaze down in wonderment on the strange faces passing to and fro. On the bosky hills around the city are the Lustschloss Fantasie, the Erimitage, a charming little garden palace, and the Rollwenzelei, where Jean Paul wrote novels. There are other memorials of this author, but now it is Wagner's name which draws pilgrims from all climes. The unsightly Wagner theatre, which looks more like a factory than a temple of art, is the first thing the traveler sees on approaching Bayreuth. Nearby is a large insane asylum, where they have cells and strait jackets reserved for the anti-Wagnerians. Farther on is a jail with a lock-up for small boys who are caught whistling anything but

"Leitmotifen." The town is Wagnerized. From the stationers' and book shop windows Wagner looks out in marble, plaster and terra cotta. His photographs and those of his artists are hawked about in the streets. Wagner cravats are to be had of all haberdashers. The happy wearer simply pulls a string and the Meister's visage pops out from under a lapel. The Wagnerian can sport a "Parsifal" hat and the Wagnerianerinnen cover their *üppige schultern* with "Nibelungen" shawls. All can drink the Meister's health in sparkling Rhinegold or Klingsor's Zaubertrank. The critic can write his review with a "Siegfried" pen.

But then this Wagner cult is perfectly natural. Wagner has given this sleepy old town a world wide fame. The Banquier finds himself honoring letters of credit on English, Russian, French and American houses. The waiter at the Sonne is scratching his head to make out "was diese Amerikaner meinen wann sie pork and beans bestellen," and an English speaking operator has been added to the telegraphic force. The people feel as though in the Wagnerian era the town would again rise to the importance it boasted during the good old days of the Margraves. Surely comparatively few Americans knew of Bayreuth before Wagner took up his abode there, built a theatre and produced the "Nibelungen Ring." Now it is more spoken of, among musical Americans at least, than Berlin, Vienna, London or Paris. Before Wagner came it was what the Germans call "ein Bauernnest;" now it is the musical centre of Germany.

Wagner doubtless selected Bayreuth from among those towns which were eager to have his theatre located within their bounds because of its somewhat secluded character. Here he could count upon a reverential spirit, with absolutely no other interest to divert it from its devotion to the Wagner cult. He himself admirably sums up the history of the place. "If," he says, "I made in ' The Mastersingers' my *Hans Sachs* eulogize Nuremburgh as lying in the centre of Germany, I thought that the same might be said still more justly of Bayreuth. The immense Hercynian forest, into which the Romans never penetrated, once extended hither. The name Frankenwald still remains, showing that the whole region was once a forest, the gradual clearing away of which is indicated in sundry local names, or made up in part of the syllables ' reuth' (*reuten*, to make a clearing). Of the name Bayreuth two different interpretations are given. According to one account, in early times the land hereabout was given to the Bavarian dukes and the Frankish king, and here the Bavarians cleared away the forest and made a home for themselves. This interpretation of the word flatters a certain historic sense of justice, in that the land, after frequent changes of owners, at last reverts to those to whom it owes a portion of its culture."

Another and more sceptical explanation would have it that " Bayreuth " is simply the name of a hamlet built up " beim Reuth " (in the clearing). However this may be, the "reuth " remains, indicating a place won from the forest, and made productive ; and here we are reminded of the " Rütli" of old Switzerland, whence the word derives a still more pleasing and more elevated significance. The land became the Frankish frontier of the German empire against the fanatical Czechs, whose more peaceable Slavic brethren had previously settled there, and so far advanced in civilization that to this day many of the names of places bear both the Slavic and the German stamp. Here first did Slavs become Germans without having to renounce their own peculiar characters ; and they peacefully share in the fortunes of the common population. This speaks well for the peculiarities of the German mind. After a long continued rule over this frontier, the Burgraves of Nuremburgh made their way into the marches of Brandenburg, where they were destined to found the kingdom of Prussia, and finally the empire of Germany. Though the Romans never penetrated hither, still Bayreuth was not uninfluenced by Roman civilization. In ecclesiastical affairs it broke boldly away from Rome. The old city, often reduced to ashes, adopted the French taste under princes with a liking for embellishment ; an Italian erected, in the shape of a grand opera house, one of the most famous monuments of the Rococo style. Here flourished ballet, opera, comedy. But the Burgomaster of Bayreuth 'affected' (as her ladyship expressed it)— 'affected to pronounce his speech of welcome to the sister of Frederick the Great in pure German.' "

" Wahnfried," Wagner's house, and the grounds in which it stands occupy about 4,500 square feet. A roadway for wagons leads straight from the gate to the front door.   Those on foot approach the house through two beautiful arbors.   Above the door is the following inscription :

| Hier wo mein wöhnen Frieden fand— | WAHNFRIED. | Sei dieses haus von mir benannt. |

expressive of the repose Wagner found here after his hopes were realized.

Under this inscription is the sgraffito drawing by Robert Krausse.   This is an allegorical drawing. Wotan, the principal figure, represents German mythology.   To the right is Greek tragedy, to the left music, and to these Siegfried looks up, the embodiment of the " Art Work of the Future."   As a stranger approached the house at the time the author was at Bayreuth three dogs sprang out of a roomy kennel and began a furious barking.   These were the Nibelungen dogs—Wotan and his wives, Freia and Fricka.   The house was built according to Wagner's own suggestions.   In the basement are the kitchen and servants' rooms ; in the cellar a furnace (this mode of heating is rather uncommon in Germany) and a capital wine cellar.   I usually dined at the restaurant where Wagner bought his wines, and I soon came to the conclusion that he knew as much about wines as he did about music.   The Leitmotif in his wine cellar was a fine array of Johannisberger, but as he was a universal genius he had not confined himself to German vineyards.

On the ground floor you enter a roomy hall which

runs clear up to the roof and receives its light from above. There are marble statues of the heroes of Wagner's operas, by Zumbusch, and two busts of the Meister by Dr. Kietz, of Dresden. The frieze is decorated with frescoes representing scenes from "Der Ring des Nibelungen." A room of about 1,500 feet square opens into this hall. The walls are for the most covered with little bric-à-brac shelves and bookcases. The latter contain a great amount of curious literature, mostly folk lore relating to the subjects on which the Meister has based the plots of his music dramas. There is also a piano in one corner. The room receives light from a large bay window. In one side of this bay window is a large tropical plant; in the other the plain table at which Wagner sat at work. There was usually nothing on the table except a few sheets of music paper and an inkstand, and on the inkstand a penholder, which looked as though the Meister had been chewing at it. The back door of this room leads into the garden.

In this room, the hall and the large dining room Frau Cosima usually received her guests. When Liszt stood beside her it was easy to see the resemblance between them. Liszt had on his face a number of huge warts, for each of which his female adorers had some pet name. These warts made his fine, strong head all the stronger looking, and he can hardly be blamed for the fact that a lot of silly women made fools of themselves over him. The same is true of Wagner, upon whom, in 1882, I saw a French authoress and other women attempting to fawn in the most open and disgusting manner. The company at the Wahnfried receptions in 1882 consisted chiefly of the artists and their friends, some German musicians and members of the Patronatsverein. At one reception there were some Englishmen present who had opera glasses through which, as they stood in the middle of the room, they examined the ceiling and walls and the company as well. Some of the pretty *Blumenmädchen* (the alluring flower girls in the second act of " Parsifal ") came in, and Liszt, whose eye for female beauty seemed undimmed, at once began to chaff them and joke with them. Wagner suddenly rushed in from a side door, threw his arms around Scaria, the basso, exclaiming : " This is for your splendid performance yesterday," kissed him and rushed out of the room again. Nearly an hour afterward he appeared again and was walking toward Liszt, who was in the middle of the room, when one of the Englishmen who had been looking through an opera glass spied him and at once made for him. " Herr Wagner," he said, in broken German, as he got near to him, "I had such a good time listening to ' Parsifal.'

Hardly had Wagner heard the words "had a good time," before he turned and darted from the room, shrieking, as he threw up his hands in dismay : "If you want to have a good time go and hear something of Offenbach's !"

That was the last seen that night of the Meister and—the Englishman.

In the evenings when there was no reception at Wahnfried there were always some of the principal singers to be found in the wine room of the Hotel Sonne. One night Materna would dress the salad and Scaria brew the punch, and the next night the rôles would be reversed. The prettiest among the *Blumenmädchen* looked after the trimmings. One evening Materna told us that Wagner had been in particularly good spirits at the theatre rehearsal that afternoon. While he was singing a certain phrase for her, to show her some particular nuance, his voice broke. Turning to Liszt and bowing apologetically he said : "Excuse me, sir ; I have not practiced my solfeggios this morning." This led Scaria to tell us an anecdote which he had from Wagner himself. When Wagner was conductor of the London Philharmonic concerts he rehearsed a Beethoven symphony from memory. As the sainted Mendelssohn, who had dined with the Queen and the Prince Consort, had always led from a score, the directors thought there must be something radically wrong in Wagner's method of procedure and remonstrated with him so strongly that he promised to conduct from the score at the concert. Accordingly that evening he had a music book on his desk and turned the leaves from time to time as he conducted the symphony. After the concert one of the directors came up to him and said : "Now, Herr Wagner, you must admit that the symphony went much better with the score than without it." Wagner calmly pointed to the score he had used. It was that of Rossini's "Barber of Seville."

This seems to be the proper point at which to introduce some of Wagner's characteristic sayings which have been reported by Von Wolzogen, Dan:. reuther and others. Speaking of a perfect balance between the means employed and the effects produced he said : " Mozart's music and Mozart's orchestra are a perfect match ; an equally perfect balance exists between Palestrina's choir and Palestrina's counterpoint ; and I find a similar correspondence between Chopin's piano and some of his etudes and preludes. I do not care for the 'ladies' Chopin,' there is too much of the Parisian salon in that.   But he has given us many things that are above the salon."

Few musical people—in this country at least—will agree with his opinion of Schumann, though Wagner on Schumann is less intolerant than Schumann on Wagner. "Schumann's peculiar treatment of the pianoforte," he said, "grates on my ear ; there is too much blur ; you cannot produce his pieces unless it be with obligato pedal. What a relief to hear a sonata of Beethoven's !   In early days I thought more would come of Schumann.   His *Zeitschrift* was brilliant and his pianoforte works showed great originality.   There was much ferment, but also much real power, and many bits are quite unique and perfect.   I think highly, too, of many of his songs, though they are not quite as great as Schubert's.   He took pains with his declamation—no small merit a generation ago.   Later on I saw a good deal of him at Dresden, but then already his head was tired, his powers on the wane.   He consulted me about the text to 'Genoveva,' which he was arranging from Tieck's and Hebbel's plays; yet he would not take my advice—he seemed to fear some trick."

Wagner was much censured for what were considered his bitter attacks upon Mendelssohn, yet he expressed unreserved admiration for several of Mendelssohn's compositions. He was especially fond of the " Hebrides " overture, calls Mendelssohn a musical landscape painter of the first order and speaks of this overture as his masterpiece. "Wonderful imagination and delicate feeling are here presented with consummate art," he said. " Note the extraordinary beauty of the passage where the oboe rises above the other instruments with a plaintive wail like sea winds over the seas ! 'Calm at Sea and Happy Voyage ' also is beautiful, and I am very fond of the first movement of the Scotch symphony. No one can blame a composer for using national melodies when he treats them so artistically as Mendelssohn has done in the scherzo of this symphony. His second themes, his slow movements generally, where the human element comes in, are weaker. As regards the overture to 'A Midsummer Night's Dream,' it must be taken into account that he wrote it at seventeen, and how finished the form is already!"

Schubert's songs he rated, as noted before, very high ; but this admiration did not extend to Schubert's other works. Nevertheless his opinion will be interesting, even to Schubert's most ardent admirers, among whom the author is happy to count himself.

"Schubert," said Wagner, "has produced model songs, but that is no reason for us to accept his pianoforte sonatas or his ensemble pieces as really solid work, not more than we need accept Weber's songs, his pianoforte quartet, or the trio with a flute, because of his wonderful operas. Schumann's enthusiasm for Schubert's trios and the like was a mystery to Mendelssohn. I remember Mendelssohn speaking to me of the note of Viennese *bonhomie* (*bürgerliche Behabligkeit*) which runs through some things of Schubert's. Curiously enough, Liszt still likes to play Schubert. I cannot account for it; that 'Divertissement à la Hongroise' verges on triviality, no matter how it is played."

Speaking of *pièces d'occasion* and with special reference to the "Centennial March," he said : "I am not a learned musician ; I never had occasion to pursue antiquarian researches, and periods of transition did not interest me much. I went straight from Palestrina to Bach, from Bach to Gluck and Mozart—or, if you choose, along the same path backward. It suited me personally to rest content with the acquaintance of the principal men, the heroes and their main works. For aught I know this may have had its drawbacks ; anyway, my mind has never been stuffed with 'music in general.' Being no learned person I have not been able to write to order. Unless the subject absorbs me completely I cannot produce twenty bars worth listening to."

To those young musicians who think they follow Wagner by devising eccentric instrumental effects the following remark will be of value :

" In instrumental music I am a *réactionnaire*, a conservative. I dislike everything that requires a verbal explanation beyond the actual sounds. For instance, the middle of Berlioz's touching ' Scène d'Amour,' in his ' Romeo and Juliet,' is meant by him to reproduce in musical phrases the lines about the lark and the nightingale in Shakespeare's balcony scene, but it does nothing of the sort ; it is not intelligible as music. Berlioz added to, altered and spoiled his work. This so-called ' Symphonie Dramatique ' of Berlioz as it now stands is neither fish nor flesh ; strictly speaking it is no symphony at all. There is no unity of matter, no unity of style. The choral recitatives, the songs and other vocal pieces have little to do with the instrumental movements. The operatic finale, *Père Laurent* especially, is a failure. Yet there are beautiful things right and left. The ' Convoi Funébre ' is very touching and a masterly piece. So, by the way, is the Offertoire of the requiem. The opening theme of the ' Scène d'Amour ' is heavenly ; the garden scene and the fête at the Capulets' enormously clever ; indeed, Berlioz was diabolically clever (*verflucht pfiffig*). I made a minute study of his instrumentation as early as 1840 at Paris, and have often taken up his scores since. I profited greatly, both as regards what to do and what to leave undone."

Regarding the efforts made to introduce his music into France, Wagner said : "Pasdeloup made every effort to acclimatize me in France and I thank him. But no one can become acquainted with me through concerts. I must be introduced at the theatre, for, to appear properly, I need not only singers but scenic effects and the entire dramatic apparatus. In my compositions all the parts are closely related, one conditioned by the others ; and if one of these is omitted the unity of my work suffers. My works, however, will never receive recognition in your country. My music is too German. I strive, with all the power given me, to be the child of my fatherland. It is also dangerous to listen to my musical declamation without the use of a text, for they are reciprocal. Why have you not in Paris an international stage, where celebrated foreign compositions can be given in the original language ? Composers would then be happy to appear before a Parisian public, which is the most intelligent in the world. I know my music is not played in Paris for other deplorably absurd reasons. Of these, however, I will no longer speak ; they belong to the past. I am supposed to be bitterly disposed toward the French. And why ? Because they hissed my 'Tannhäuser ?' Is it certain that it was heard correctly ? Auber could answer for me ; into his ear I whispered my woes. The moment for earnest music had not then arrived. As regards the journalists, I cannot complain of them all. I did not visit them as did Meyerbeer ; yet Baudelaire, Champfleury and Schuré have written the best articles on my works that have appeared. I am not as dissatisfied with Paris as report says."

The best view I had of Wagner was at a dinner given by him to his artists and a few friends at the restaurant near the Wagner Theatre. At one end of this restaurant the floor was sunk considerably and steps led down to it. In this space was the table for the composer and his guests. A dinner was served on the upper portion to which, on payment, anyone was admitted, so that whoever chose to pay for the dinner could also have the pleasure of watching the proceedings in the pit. Wagner and his guests dined to a full house. The composer was the last to appear on the scene, entering hastily. This was the first time I saw him and I must own I was greatly disappointed in his looks. He was in spick and span clothes—something unpardonable in a genius. A light overcoat, gray trousers and lavender gloves were the most conspicuous details of his costume. He was undersized and walked with short, quick steps, Altogether he looked like a little dandy. But when he took off his hat and revealed his grand forehead his genius was impressively apparent. Looking up from the elect to where the spectators sat he exclaimed, somewhat contemptuously: " Da is ja auch das Publikum " (There are also the lookers on). Wagner treated his audiences, and even admirers who were nearer to him, pretty much as a father would his bad children.

After dinner there were speeches. Some local dignitaries made long and uninteresting remarks. Wagner's address was brief, but snappy and to the point. In its course he said some nice things about father-in-law Liszt. Wagner sat between his wife and Liszt, and concluded with a fine tribute to his artists. " I am," he said, " under deep obligations to all who have contributed to the fund for the ' Parsifal ' performances, but I am under deeper obligations to my

artists ; for, after all, art is not created by money but
by artists."

I saw Wagner again after the first and last acts of
" Parsifal."   After the curtains closed on the first act
the audience broke out into loud applause and called
for Wagner.   The enthusiasm not subsiding, he came
out and scolded " das Publikum " roundly, saying that
this was not a theatrical performance and that they
ought to be ashamed of themselves for thinking of
recalls before the end of the last act.   " Das Publikum "
forthwith meekly subsided, and during the rest of the
performance was decorously *weihevoll* and *verklärt.*
After the last act, however, the artists and Wagner
were called before the curtain, the composer thank-
ing his artists much in the same language which he
had employed at the dinner.   " Das Publikum," however, which had contributed the shekels was not
thanked.   Aside from the performances at Bayreuth,
there was something about the Wagner cult as practiced there which struck a cool headed American
newspaper man—even if he was a Wagnerite—as very
funny.

The performance, however, left an indelible impression upon me, and by it as a standard I have
measured all Wagnerian representations which I have
heard since then.   None of them has come up to
that production of " Parsifal ; " for not only the
work itself but the performance also bore the stamp
of Wagner's genius.   He personally superintended
the arduous rehearsals, gave the most minute directions regarding the *mise en scène* and instructed the

artists in the execution of the music and in the stage business.

Soon after the curtain had risen on this production of " Parsifal," my attention was suddenly attracted by a peculiar excrescence on one of the rocks in the left foreground of the stage. Gradually, as I looked, the excrescence assumed the shape of a human head, and some minutes afterward I was able to distinguish the face of Wagner himself outlined against the piece of rock scenery. At first I supposed he had ventured out too far from behind the scenes in order to observe the effect of his last music drama upon the audience. But this supposition was dispelled by the circumstance that he rarely looked toward the auditorium. He seemed rather to be watching the singers on the stage. The face remained in view until the panoramic change of scene from the forest to the Castle of the Grail. It struck me as a curious circumstance that although I frequently looked at the face during the progress of the scene, it did not grow into any bolder relief against the rock, but remained almost as flat as though it had been painted into the scenery.

Afterward I asked a number of friends in the audience if they had seen what I had. They had not, nor had others of whom they made inquiries. I was beginning to think that the appearance of Wagner's face against the rock was a freak of mirage, resulting perhaps from the positions of some of the lights behind the scenes, when I mentioned the matter to one of the principal singers in the cast. He manifested surprise, not at what I had discovered, but at my having discovered it. He then told me that weeks before the production of " Parsifal " Wagner had chalked little crosses on the stage to indicate the exact spots where he wanted the singers to stand, and had also drawn lines to show the direction in which they were to move from one point to another, and had himself drilled them in every movement. At the dress rehearsals and during the performance he had watched them, except during the first scene of the first act, from behind the scenes, in order to observe whether or not they closely followed his directions.

Discovering that in the scene referred to he could not command a full view of the stage from any point at which he was entirely hidden from the audience, he had selected the place where I had noticed him, because there, when the stage was lighted, his complexion and the coloring of the scenery almost blended, and he considered himself safe from detection. I was much impressed at this incident. For it furnished a clue to the vast amount of labor which, unknown to the public, preceded the production of " Parsifal." If one detail in the performance had necessitated so much thought, drilling and watchfulness, how much of these, beyond the most liberal estimate of the public, must have been developed during the long period of preparation !

One of the most impressive incidents of the production was the reverential spirit in which the audience followed the work. The cult which had so

many ridiculous features outside the walls of the
Wagner Theatre was an element of beauty within
them. The performance in consequence progressed
without the slightest disturbance from the auditorium
except the occasional hissing of extreme Wagnerites
at some fancied sacrilege, such as the rustling of a
programme. Just before the beginning of the *Vorspiel*
the doors were closed and no one was admitted until
the end of the first act. The rule was enforced
with equal rigor during the second and third
acts. Therefore there was no disturbance from late
comers. They paid the penalty of their lack of punc-
tuality by being obliged to wait until the act upon which
the doors had closed was over. The lights in the auditorium were lowered and, as the orchestra was sunk
out of sight, there was no long haired Capellmeister
to draw attention from the performance to his own
gymnastics, and no bowing and blowing of orchestral
players to watch. The *Vorspiel* certainly produced a
most *spirituel* effect, its ethereal harmonies rising like
perfume from an "unseen censer;" and when the curtains parted the stage monopolized the attention of
all.

The scene disclosed by the parting of the curtain
was calculated to heighten the *spirituel* effect produced by the *Vorspiel*. It was an exquisite forest
vista awakening to the first delicate touches of the
morning sun. One could peer between gray columns
into deep recesses shaded by soft green arches. The
ground was uneven, little mounds and hollows and
a rocky ascent in the background adding to the

natural appearance of the scenery. The light effect was most beautiful, very soft, like that of approaching day, and hardly casting a shadow. The scene was not the ordinary "set," but was largely composed of separate trees, with branches and leaves cut out so as to give most effectively the idea of a real forest. Between these branches and leaves a network was hung, and this with the soft light gave a hazy atmospheric effect. This device is now frequently applied, and can be witnessed at almost any performance at the Metropolitan Opera House, but at the time it was quite new, having been introduced, I believe, in 1876, at the Bayreuth Theatre.

Added to this atmospheric effect was a gentle swaying of the leaves and branches, as if a gentle breeze was passing through the forest. Grouped under a huge tree in the foreground were *Gurnemanz* and two pages, the one a vigorous old knight, the other two exceedingly graceful and pretty youths. At the signal from the castle the knight slowly awakened and called to the pages, who yawned and finally opened their eyes. This was all done in a very natural manner, and in fact all the effects produced during this performance seemed to have the one aim in view—to simulate nature. A word is due these pages and all others who took the parts of pages in this scene and in the processions and of flower girls in the second act. They were exceedingly pretty and graceful, and had, been selected by Wagner, who was a connoisseur in such matters, for these very attributes.

It is, of course, impossible to analyze every feature of the performance. This could not be done without at the same time analyzing the work itself, and as an analysis of " Parsifal " is given in Volume II. of this work, I can here only reproduce the most striking features of the representation. As the morning brightened the light gradually increased in power. The first decided break upon the calm was the wild entrance of *Kundry* in her savage garb, girdled with a snake's skin, her black hair streaming in the wind and her eyes gleaming with a fierce fire. As she lay upon the ground looking at the knight and pages she resembled more some savage animal of the forest than a woman. The scene became more animated when *Amfortas* was borne in upon his litter, followed by his knights and pages. They were clad in blue and red, colors which contrasted very effectively with the soft hues of the forest. Excellent, too, was the gradual disappearance of the procession, as the king was borne down the depression toward the lake.

Another striking dramatic effect was produced when *Gurnemanz's* narrative of the misfortunes which had fallen upon the knighthood was interrupted by sudden cries from the lake, and the wounded swan fluttered upon the scene and fell at the old knight's feet, *Parsifal* being immediately afterward led in a captive. When *Gurnemanz* uttered his noble reproof, at the same time gently holding up the swan to *Parsifal's* gaze, the bird gently lifted its neck and wings in the last motions before death. Very striking, too, was the panoramic effect when *Gurnemanz* conducted *Parsifal* to the castle. The four heavy sets of scenery were

drawn off simultaneously toward the right, and the
drop during which the final change took place was
lowered for so short a time that the characters
seemed to pass almost directly out of the rocky cav-
ern into which they were last seen disappearing into
the great hall of the castle.

This last was a beautiful interior of white, blue and
gold, with long colonnades extending far into the
background and a beautiful dome in the centre. One
seemed to be actually standing in the hall and looking
up into this dome almost to its roof. The religious
service which followed was of a deeply devotional
character, and certainly I have never heard in any
church service an effect more spiritual than was produced by the boys' voices which floated down from
the dome. It seemed as if every note were a dove-
winged thought of religious faith. This was clearly
the most beautiful effect produced during the entire
performance, and it has been said that agnostics who
have attended the performances of "Parsifal" have
actually felt for the first time the influence of religious
faith during this scene.

The second act also opened in an architectural structure, but of such different construction as to form of
itself a dramatic contrast. In this scene *Klingsor*, the
magician, summons *Kundry* before him, and, when
Parsifal is seen approaching the magic garden, by a
wave of his spear causes the structure to vanish and
the garden to take its place. This change was
wrought with lightning speed, the castle vanishing
as if it had been swallowed up by the earth. In place

of the sombre walls was a garden filled with huge flowers of garish colors. The effect was at first almost painful to the eye, but afterward the dramatic necessity for these exaggerated hues was apparent, for when *Klingsor* hurled the spear at *Parsifal*, and the latter, seizing it, made a sign of the cross and thereby changed the garden into a howling waste, the dreariness of this desert was enhanced by contrast with the bright colors of the garden. This change was another wonderful effect, everything being done so quickly that the flowers actually seemed to wither before the eyes of the spectators. The spear, it will be remembered, when it is hurled by *Klingsor* remains suspended over *Parsifal*. This mechanical effect is produced by having the weapon hung to an invisible wire, over which it slides by a loop, its swift course toward *Parsifal* being checked by an obstacle on the wire directly over *Parsifal's* head. He then simply reaches up for the spear, and by a quick gesture tears it off from its hanging.

The first scene of the last act was also in the forest and the effects were of similar beauty to those described in the forest scene in which the work opened, the final scene being again the hall of the castle.

The artists who enacted this work were Wagner's own choice. The part of *Parsifal* was sung alternately by Winkelman and Gudehus. These are both gifted actors and singers, and there is little to be said of either as against the other. Both simply did their parts admirably. *Kundry* was taken by Materna, Brandt and Malten. Of these three the last named best realized the ideal of *Kundry* in the second act when she appears as a beautiful, seductive woman. The two others in this scene hardly came up to Wagner's conception, as they lacked the necessary beauty of features. When Wagner requested Brandt to take the part of *Kundry* and when the latter realized that a beautiful woman was required to do the part justice in the second act, she wrote to Wagner that she did not think she had the necessary good looks. Wagner answered : " What I want is artistic feeling. Rouge and costume will do the rest."

Brandt therefore accepted, but she afterward had reason to regret the choice, as her experience at Bayreuth was unpleasant, Wagner showing his preference for Materna and Malten in a manner which, to say the least, was not very gallant toward a devoted artist. In the first and second acts Materna and Brandt were fully equal to the exacting demands of the character. Reichman was an admirable *Amfortas*. But the most striking performance was undoubtedly the *Gurnemanz* of Scaria, a noble creation, resonant musically and dramatically finished to the last detail, a perfect example of musical and dramatic art. This is really the only individual performance which stood out in bold relief against the rest, and perhaps it may be as much due to the striking character which Wagner drew as to the merits of the artist, for all engaged in this performance seemed devoted to the one idea, as grand as it is rare, of reproducing with the utmost fidelity the intentions of the poet and the composer. The difficult choruses were given in

Behind the Scenes.

The Siegfried Dragon.

LOHENGRIN & HIS SWAN CAR.

a flawless manner and so was the orchestral portion of the work.

I have touched upon several of the ingenious mechanical properties used in " Parsifal." Probably the reader will be interested in a description of three other important Wagnerian properties—the " Lohengrin" swan and the " Siegfried" dragon and forge. These were described in a fully illustrated article, " Behind the Scenes of an Opera House," which I contributed to *Scribner's Magazine* of October, 1888 (Vol. IV., No. 4), the description being here reproduced with the permission of Messrs. Charles Scribner's Sons. The illustrations which accompanied the article were after photographs taken by me behind the scenes of the Metropolitan Opera House, Mr. Stanton, the managing director, courteously placing every facility at my disposal. The drawings of the swan, dragon and forge in this book are after other photographs taken by me at the same time.

The " Lohengrin" swan, as at present constructed, is the result of the survival of the fittest, its evolution having proceeded on the lines of the principle that a mechanical property should be so constructed that it can be worked by the smallest possible number of men. Formerly the miniature figures of the swan and *Lohengrin* having been drawn across the background, the knight of the Holy Grail and his ornithological motor suddenly emerged from behind one of the wings directly back of the river's bank and moved half way across the stage. There *Lohengrin* disembarked and sang his " Farewell, my faithful swan ! "

The latest improvement was devised in order that
the swan might have the appearance of swimming
down the winding stream.   At the same time the apparatus was so constructed that it could be worked
by only two men.   The shell-like craft in which *Lohengrin* stands was built upon a three wheeled truck, the
top of which was just concealed by the set piece representing the bank of the Scheldt.   Under this truck
sat two men in positions which enabled them to place
their feet on the floor and thus shove the truck along,
the man over the front wheel steering by means of a
rod connected with this wheel.   The swan is supported
by two rods running out from the front of the truck.

The neck of the swan is "built" around a steel
spring ; the body and wings are feathers and swan's
down upon wire work.   It will be remembered that
while *Lohengrin* sings his farewell the swan gracefully
inclines its head and gently spreads its wings.   The
former motion is produced by a thin fishing line
which is attached to the swan's beak and pulled by
one of the men under the truck.   The wings work by
a clock movement.   In the last act of "Lohengrin '
the swan sinks from view—it is transformed into *Elsa's* brother—and a dove flutters in front of the boat
as it bears the knight homeward.   This change is ef-
fected very simply.   The rods upon which the swan
rests work on hinges and are held in position by two
lines drawn taut by one of the men under the truck,
who at the proper moment slackens the line, causing
the rods to drop by the weight of the swan, which
sinks out of sight.

The man sitting near the front wheel then shoves out a rod to the end of which a mechanical dove is attached, it and the curved end of the rod having been concealed behind the prow of *Lohengrin's* shell-like little craft. When "Lohengrin" was first given at Her Majesty's, London, an attempt was made to introduce this apparatus. It was duly rehearsed, but at the performance the set-water strips were placed too near the bank, so cramping the truck's steering room that it crashed into the bank. Campanini, who was the *Lohengrin*, dropped sword and shield, and facing the audience shouted : "There's stage management for you !"

For the production of "Siegfried" at the Metropolitan Opera House a dragon was designed and manufactured which the German artists declare to be the most practical and impressive monster they have seen. The head of this dragon is of papier maché. The body, 30 feet long, is of thin wire covered with curled leather scales, which are bronzed and painted. This monster, in spite of its size, is worked by a boy who is the dragon's front legs. He is dressed in a suit of canvas painted the color of the dragon's hide and having curled leather scales on the trousers below the knees, his shoes being the huge clawed feet. He gets into the dragon behind its head, which conceals him from the waist up, his legs being the dragon's front legs.

With his hands he opens and closes its huge mouth and shoves its eyelids over its eyes when it expires. The steam which it breathes out is supplied through an elastic pipe which, entering at the tail, runs through to the throat. The scene lasts about forty minutes and is very exhausting to the front legs.

In Germany the artist who sings the dragon's part is inside the hide and sings through a speaking trumpet. At the Metropolitan Opera House the artist sits under the raised bridge upon which the dragon is placed and sings through a speaking trumpet. His music is on a stand, a stage hand throws the light of a lamp upon it, and the solo répétiteur gives him his cues from the wings. The voice sounds as though it issued through the dragon's throat. The advantage of this arrangement is that it places in the monster a person whose attention is concentrated upon working this mechanical property in the best possible manner. The dragon when not in commission is stabled in mid-air under the paint bridge. The day of the performance it is lowered by ropes, thoroughly groomed, and then allowed to stretch itself out upon the floor against the rear wall and lie there until the end of the first act.

The first act of "Siegfried" depends for its picturesqueness more on the successful management of the gas effects than on any other element of the performance. To "gas" this act is an exceedingly difficult problem, for in its course a great variety of light effects are introduced, a number of them simultaneously. For instance, no less than three different kinds of lighting come into play together every time *Siegfried* in the forging scene fans the fire with the bellows. In theatrical parlance the bellows "has to be practically gassed;" which means that the flaring up of the fire

Swaytingata Tongs behind the Scenes.

and its fitful gleaming upon the surrounding objects must be imitated. The manner in which these effects were produced is shown in the illustration of the rear view of the forge. This forge is a framework, the front, sides and top being covered. Sunk into the top is a space for a gas jet, a piece of split gas pipe and a tube leading into a box immediately underneath, which is filled with lycopodium powder. A person lying under the forge takes a rubber tube, which leads from this box into his mouth.

On the forge is a box painted to resemble a stone. In it are six incandescent electric lights behind a piece of red gelatine. The wire for these runs from a "pocket" in the wing. Near this is also the gas pocket from which the tube for supplying the gas jet and split pipe issues and runs along the stage to the hearth. The gas jet is lighted before the curtain rises. In the wings a man with a mirror stands near an electric light. What occurs when *Siegfried* pulls the handle of the bellows is as follows :

A man in the wings turns a cock admitting the gas to the tube which feeds the split pipe. The gas when it reaches the split is ignited by the burning jet. At the same time the man under the forge blows through the tube which leads into the box of lycopodium powder. A quantity of this volatile powder is thus blown up out of the box. Coming in contact with the jet and the flames from the split pipe, it blazes up, the ignited particles at the same time floating over the hearth and thus producing the effect of gaseous flames flickering over a bed of coal or embers

and running in lambent undulations from the point
at which the current from the bellows fanned the fire.
The man who turns on the gas makes at the same
time electrical connection with the box of incandescent lights, and these shining through the red gelatine throw a red glare upon *Siegfried*. At the same
time the man with the mirror so manipulates it that
the reflection of the electric light runs up and down
the wing behind *Siegfried*.

In addition to the lights in the scene of the forging of the sword there are several independent light
effects in this act. Among these are the glints of sun-
shine which play through the foliage of the forest
back of *Mime's* dwelling, and which inspire his terror-
ized mind with so much dread after the *Wanderer's*
direful prophecy. To produce this effect here and in
the *Waldweben* scene of the next act two panels of
hammered white glass glazed with lead in irregular
shapes (one of them arranged on a pin so that it can
be slid sidewise over the other and back again) are
held in front of an electric light, the sliding panel being moved rapidly to and fro. Then there are the
lights thrown on *Wotan*, the sunlight in the forest,
and the white light thrown on *Siegfried* just before
the curtain goes down.

WAGNER'S WRITINGS.

WAGNER'S WRITINGS.

INTRODUCTORY.

WAGNER'S "Collected Literary Works" are contained in ten stout volumes—a formidable
library, both as regards size and the character of its
contents. Few even of his most ardent admirers are
familiar with these writings as a whole ; nor is such
familiarity necessary to an intelligent appreciation of
his art theories. His system can be explained in far
more concise language than he has employed, for his
language is anything but concise. It is often obscure
and diffuse. Indeed a translator of Wagner's technical essays is usually obliged to first translate them
into German—that is, from Wagnerian German into
good German.

His most important technical essays relating to his
own art theories are : " Das Kunstwerk der Zukunft "
(The Art Work of the Future) ; " Oper und Drama "
(Opera and Drama) ; " Zukunftsmusik " (' The Music of
the Future '—the inverted commas show that the
term did not originate with Wagner ; in fact he

quoted it from a hostile critic) ; " Ueber die Anwend-
ung der Musik auf das Drama " (Music in its Relations to the Drama).   Other technical works, more
clearly and interestingly written than those relating
to his art theories, are analyses of Beethoven's
" Eroica," ninth symphony and " Coriolanus " overture and his own " Flying Dutchman," and " Tannhäuser " overtures and the *Vorspiel* to " Lohengrin,"
and on conducting ; and related to this class of his
writings the famous polemic " Das Judenthum in der
Musik " (Judaism in Music).   Several of his miscel-
laneous writings are fine literary productions.   Indeed it may be said that the further he got away from
technical matters the more facile he grew with the
pen.

The novelettes written during his residence in Paris
(1840 and 1841) are highly successful, especially the
tragic tale " An End in Paris."   It contains the famous
musical creed : " I believe in God, Mozart and Beethoven and in their disciples and apostles ! "   An autobiographical sketch (to 1841) and reminiscences of
Rossini, Auber, Spohr and Spontini are also brightly
written ; but probably the American lay reader is not
very deeply interested in the subjects of the reminiscences.   The essay on Beethoven is metaphysical,
with all that term implies when applied to a German
essay. His dramatic poems and a letter on Liszt's Symphonic Poems are also embraced in his " Collected
Literary Works."   There is, besides these published
writings, a privately printed autobiography continuing
the sketch referred to above.

Edward L. Burlinghame, under the title of "Art Life and Theories of Richard Wagner" (in the Amateur Series, Henry Holt & Co., New York), has translated the "Autobiography" (the sketch to 1841), "The Love Veto, the Story of the First Performance of an Opera," "A Pilgrimage to Beethoven," "An End in Paris," "'Der Freischütz' in Paris," "The Music of the Future," "An Account of the Production of 'Tannhäuser' in Paris," "The Purpose of the Opera," "Musical Criticism," and "The Opera House at Bayreuth." Hueffer has translated the letter on Liszt's Symphonic Poems, and Dannreuther the essays "Beethoven," "The Music of the Future" and "On Conducting." Nothing in the "Collected Literary Works," both of those translated into English and remaining untranslated, compares in interest with the "Correspondence of Wagner and Liszt," which is frequently quoted in the biographical portion of this work.

The author is of the opinion that Wagner's theory of the true relations between music and drama is best set forth by analysis of his music dramas with the leading motives given in musical notation. He has pursued this course in the second volume of this work, and he believes that the lay reader will gain therefrom a better comprehension of the theory and method upon which Wagner proceeded than from the poet-composer's writings on the subject. He has, however, selected for translation that essay from the "Collected Literary Works" which appears to him the most clearly expressed and to be most likely to interest the lay reader—"Music in its Relations to the

Drama. So far as he is aware no other English translation of it exists.

MUSIC IN ITS RELATIONS TO THE DRAMA.

My last essay on the opera closed with the suggestion that there exist certain essential and inherent
differences between symphonic music and operatic
composition, or purely orchestral music and music
when it enters into combination with the drama.
This suggestion I would like to use now as a leading
thought ; because I consider the subject to which it
refers of sufficient importance to merit an extended
examination, especially as it will have a tendency to
enlighten or correct the views of some of our operatic composers. In my last communication I mentioned certain "bunglers" who take, without reason,
unnecessary liberties with the muse, and others who
regard with terror every act which conflicts with their
traditionary ideas of decorum. The latter I stigma-
tized as "senators." This euphemistic expression for
an epithet derived from the animal kingdom I have
from *Iago*, who, when *Brabantio* says to him, "Thou
art an ass," simply replies, "Thou art—a senator."
Iago's respect for one of high political rank led him to
substitute one term for the other, and with somewhat similar respect for scientific dignitaries I shall
henceforward use the term "professor."

But to return to our subject. As an illustration of
the difference in the musical styles of which I am
treating I point at the outset, as an important example in the history of my art, to the fact that Beet-

hoven, who was so daring in his symphonies, appears anxious and hesitating in "Fidelio." He found the outlines of operatic composition clearly defined ; and I have previously expressed my conviction that he felt uncomfortable in such narrow limits, and was therefore unwilling to attempt the dramatic style more than once. That he should not have remoulded the proportions of operatic composition with the pressure of his powerful mind can be explained only by assuming that he was sufficiently employed in reconstructing the symphonic form, and that his craving for independence was satisfied by new departures in his purely instrumental works. And if we give close attention to the abundant fruits of these labors, we must acknowledge that Beethoven defined the plastic limits of orchestral music so clearly that even his own impulsive genius dared not overleap them. Yet we must regard these limits as conditions, required by the very nature of the system to which they are applied, rather than as hindering barriers. These plastic conditions are columns which give the symphonic structure firmness, consistency and clearly defined proportions.

Beethoven hesitated to alter the fundamental forms of the symphony as it had been transmitted by Haydn, just as an architect hesitates to move the columns of a building or to confuse what is horizontal and vertical. If the structure was conventional it naturally required this conventionality. The form of music called symphony is developed from the dance rhythm. It is impossible for me to repeat all I have

said and proved elsewhere on this very subject. I
can only point to what I consider the germ of the
Haydn and Beethoven symphony.   This origin ex-
cludes dramatic pathos, so that the most active complications of symphonic themes are never analogous
to dramatic action, and can be regarded only as combinations of ideal dance measures, independent of
verse or rhetoric.   Here is not purpose or consum-
mation, but for this reason dignified enjoyment only.
Radically different melodies are never placed in opposition ; however great the contrast may appear,
they are reciprocal, like the male and female of the
same species.   But what a varied life these elements
lead, how they may be separated for a while, how one
may be forced from the other and then both reunited
in passionate embrace—all this is portrayed in a single symphonic movement of Beethoven's ; so vividly,
indeed, as for instance in the first movement of the
"Eroica," that, while it appears doubly clear to the
initiated, the uninitiated may be misled.

I think I may affirm with justice that whoever endeavors to merge music in tragedy, or to use it with
true dramatic effect, will face different conditions ;
conditions of whose requirements, as opposed to
those of the symphonic school, he should give faithful account.   Talented composers for the orchestra,
who have sought to break through the barriers which
hem in the traditionary form of instrumental music,
have given their works certain titles and have allowed
music alone to portray the dramatic action suggested
thereby.   That these efforts can never result in the

ideal work of art has, I think, been frequently admitted, but nevertheless the composers who have made these attempts have not been mere idle dreamers, and the real, practical value of their labors has not as yet been fully acknowledged. The vagaries in which the demon that presided over the genius of Berlioz delighted assume, when reflected by the subtly artistic disposition of Liszt, innumerable physical and psychological proportions ; so that it seemed to his disciples as though an entirely novel species of composition had been placed at their disposal.

It was at any rate astonishing to note with what elasticity music began to yield to the pressure of dramatic action. Before that time the overture to an opera or to theatrical pieces was the only substitute for the pure symphonic form. But in using this substitute composers proceeded with the greatest caution. Beethoven, for instance, after a purely theatrical effect in the middle of the "Leonore" overture, repeats the first part of the composition with the usual changes of key, unmindful of the fact that the hearer who is susceptible to dramatic influences would find the repetition inconsistent with dramatic purpose. Weber, in his overture to "Der Freischütz," was more consistent. After the intermediate movement of his work he reaches the conclusion by a compact and powerful thematic collision. And although we find in the most ambitious examples of programme music by the modern composers I spoke of above lines of the symphonic form which cannot be obliterated, their themes, harmonies and

modulations have that passionate and eccentric character which they and their followers are obliged to
adopt if they wish to portray as vividly as possible
the poetic or dramatic figure floating before their
eyes—characteristics which the symphonists pretend
to abhor. When afterward the composers began
to imagine words and gestures and to express these
by means of instrumental recitatives, and when
critics protested in holy horror against this dissolu-
tion of form, nothing remained but to construct of
the various elements a new form—that of the music
drama.

This new form differs as much from the old-fashioned opera as it does from the classical symphony.
But before we cast more light on this subject let us
glance at the works of those modern musicians who
claim to have followed in the footsteps of classical
composers, or, as they express it themselves, have
"remained classical." Whenever I listen to the compositions of these modern "classicists" I seem to
hear constant repetitions of the phrase, "We would if
we could." Programme music, which "we" looked at
askance, brought so many thematic and harmonic
novelties and so many theatrical and pictorial effects (in landscape and even in history) which were
vividly portrayed by means of improved method in
orchestration, that only a Beethoven could have
added interesting items to the repertory of classical
symphony. "We" were silent. When at last "we"
ventured to move "our" lips symphonically "we"
began as soon as "we" noticed that "we" were

becoming turgid and tedious to decorate "ourselves" with feathers of the programme petrel. In "our" symphonies, therefore, "we" present catastrophe and melancholy; "we" are at first gloomy and sad, then bold and adventurous; "we" strive to realize the dreams of youth; but some demon throws stumbling blocks in "our" way; at last "we" extract the sharp tooth of melancholy and, laughing humorously, display the bleeding gum.

All this is considered by Hungarians and Scotchmen thorough, hardy and honest; but by others it is thought tedious. After candid examination I cannot believe that the symphonic muse has gained much from the efforts of her modern disciples. Above all must I protest against their symphonies being considered legacies of Beethoven; for, although they may have stolen his melodies, they could not plagiarize his spirit. But it is not easy for the scholars of our conservatories to understand the difference in form that exists between the classical symphonies and those of the composers who "remain classical;" for their instruction regarding " æsthetic forms " consists in learning a number of names by heart, without being obliged to cultivate their judgment by instituting comparisons.

The composers I refer to, and whom I may call classical romanticists, differ from the wild stock of programme musicians in that they seem themselves sadly in need of a programme, and make use of certain tenacious melodies, which belong properly to chamber music, and were conceived and nurtured long ago in artistic seclusion. **This** seclusion the classical romanticists have exchanged for the concert hall ; what was formerly used for quintettes and the like is now served up as a symphony ; melodic chaff, to be prepared as tea for the melancholy, who have faith in any article which is marked ''genuine.'' As a general thing, however, modern composers have given us seeming eccentricities which are explained by the underlying program. Mendelssohn, with delicate feeling, introduced his impressions of nature and traced in music what may be called an epic landscape. He had traveled much and had brought home sketches which others could not obtain. Nowadays the smooth genre paintings of local exhibitions are set to music and are supposed to justify strange instrumental effects, which at present are easily produced, and astonishing harmonies, with which familiar melodies are distorted, in order that they may not be recognized ; and all this is presented as real instrumental music.

These preliminary observations establish the following propositions : Instrumental music was no longer satisfied to be under the control of the traditional symphonic form, and sought freedom in poetical representations ; whatever reacted against this could not warm the classical features into life, and found it necessary to distort them by casting them in a strange mould. If the new departure increased the capabilities of musical expression it also proved that, if these capabilities were to be increased still further, music must turn to the drama for sup-

port, without which it would soon terminate in dis-
astrous chaos. What had remained unspoken was
now to be clearly expressed, and at the same time
the opera was to be released from hereditary slavery.
In speaking of the music drama we will proceed to
give a clear account of how music may be capable of
an infinite number of noble, artistic forms.

According to æsthetics, unity is the most important element in a work of art. This abstract unity it
is difficult to define in words, and false interpretation
of it has often led to serious errors. It is most clearly
defined in a complete work of art itself; for a work
of art owes to its unity those symmetrical proportions which hold our attention and awaken our sympathy. This perfection is most frequently observed
in the living representation of a great drama; and
therefore we do not hesitate to pronounce the great
drama the most perfect work of art. Its very opposite is the old-fashioned opera; because, in pretend-
ing to use the drama, it resolved that essential unity
into small, detached fragments known as arias. As a result we find in the opera separate pieces of short duration, which, by superficial résumé of principal and
subordinate themes, return, repetition and coda, sug-
gest the form of a symphonic movement, but which
bear no relation whatever to one another. For this
reason Beethoven is seen turning disdainfully from
the narrow limits of the operatic fragment, because
the symphony offers broader and more copious treatment of the same form.

Here we recognize at a glance that unity which af-

fects us so powerfully in the drama—a result which is
weakened as soon as strange elements begin to make
their appearance.   These strange elements began to
appear when symphonists attempted dramatic effects,
because these effects require more elastic proportions
than those of the symphony, which, as before stated,
originated in the exceedingly narrow mould of the
dance rhythm.   Yet the new form of dramatic music
requires, in order to be a work of art, that very unity
which prevails throughout the classical symphony ;
and music complies with this condition only when it
enters into the most intimate relations with the drama
as a whole, rather than with a few elements of its own
arbitrary choosing.   Such unity will result in a work of
art whose constituent parts are leading motives, which,
like those of the symphonic movement, collide, recip-
rocate, renew their form, separate and reunite.   But
the order in which all this occurs is governed in the
music drama by dramatic action, while in the symphony it is controlled by the progression of the dance.

Concerning the new form of musical composition in
its relation to the drama, I think I have said enough
elsewhere and with sufficient distinctness to enable
others to criticise, justly and with benefit to themselves, the forms which in my music I have adapted
from the drama.   I have not been followed ; and I am
reminded of only one young friend who has employed
leading motives more for their dramatic effect than
with a view to constructing a new musical period.   On
the other hand, I have experienced that in musical in-
stitutions pupils are warned against the confusedness

of my style, and that young composers, after a hasty glance at my scores, try to imitate me before they understand me. The state only pays professors who do not teach my theories ; for instance, Josef Rheinberger, in Munich (probably that their champion may be near my field of action), instead of founding liberal professorships. The latter I can hope for only in America and England ; and for this reason I will content myself at present with pointing out what portions of my scores the young composers I spoke of should study and assimilate.

I would at the outset caution those who have been educated in the schools of the classical romanticists to avoid, when they first attempt the dramatic style, unusual harmonic and instrumental effects, before a sufficient cause justifies their agency. Berlioz never felt more insulted than when musicians brought him all sorts of eccentric scores for inspection, hoping they would be praised by the composer of the "Witches' Sabbath" and such like. Liszt used to send away these musical nuisances with the remark that he did not like to be treated to cigar ashes and sawdust moistened with aqua regia. I never knew a young composer who did not expect me to sanction his eccentricities. From this I perceived that they were utterly regardless of the ever increasing care I take to avoid unnecessary harmonies and modulations. In the introduction to my "Rhinegold," for instance, I found it impossible to depart from the principal key, because there existed no reason for such a departure. A great part of the following scene between *Alberich*

and the *Rhinedaughters*, which is not wholly devoid
of action, had to be written in an intimate key, because here passion is expressed with primitive simplicity.

On the other hand, I do not deny I should have employed in the scene where *Donna Anna* appears clutch-
ing in extreme passion the betrayer *Don Juan*
stronger colors than Mozart thought justifiable, before he had enriched the conventional forms of operatic expression. He was satisfied with a certain
simplicity which I remembered when I introduced the
" Walküre " with a storm and *Siegfried* with a passage
which, containing certain themes modeled after motives in the preceding scores, brought the hearer
gradually to the solitary smithy of *Nibelheim*. Here
were the elements from which the drama was to be
developed. Something further was required by the
introduction to the scene between the sisters of fate
in the "Götterdämmerung." Here the fates of the
primeval world are twisted and wound until even the
fibres of the rope which the mysterious sisters are
seen swinging round and round as the curtain rises
twist and wind with the complications of the universe.
For this reason the introduction had to awaken feelings of anxious expectation ; and, though it required
concise treatment, it afforded opportunity to reproduce themes from the first three scores of the tetralogy, clothed with richer harmonies. But it is important how one begins.

Had I constructed an overture on the theme which
accompanies the transmission of the government of

the world from *Wotan* to the ruler of the Nibelungen-hort, I should, according to my notions, have made a most insane effort. But when I choose two simple motives, one of them the *Naturmotiv*, the other the theme through which *Walhalla* appears in the glow of the early morn, and allow them to participate in the drama with ever increasing passion, I can express with the proper use of strange harmonies the feelings of the sorrow stricken god better even than if I had chosen the theme I first mentioned. I am, however, conscious that I did not seek to thrust these strange harmonies upon my hearers as mere eccentricities, or for the sake of appearing bold. On the contrary, I endeavored by a retard in tempo and by carefully balanced dynamics to render the harmonic progressions as natural as possible, that I might retain the sympathy of the audience instead of breaking in rudely upon the sanctity of their feelings. For this reason I am opposed to productions of my operas unless they take place under my own supervision, because many Capellmeisters, by disregarding such combinations as should be carefully considered, by hurried tempos and by neglect of proper equipoise, have rendered my works unintelligible and, to some "professors," even repulsive.

The foregoing example can be applied to my music dramas generally. In addition thereto I may call attention to the numerous changes in the Motive of the Rhinedaughters, when they swim around the glittering "Rhinegold," with exclamations of childlike joy. By following this unusually simple theme in all

its changes, when the action of the drama calls successively for its combination with almost every
motive of the tetralogy, the careful student will
find an example of the variations of which the music
drama admits ; and he will also note how the variations of this motive differ from those of our classic
masters, which we view in quick succession and
varied colors as through a musical kaleidoscope. This
delicious effect was weakened as soon as strange elements crept into the original symphonic form. These
elements were introduced with a view to dramatic results ; but they developed into a weak imitation,
whose style was blurred and whose individuality was
unintelligible.

Not even those musicians who handle counterpoint
with the greatest ease, whose imagination calls up the
most fantastic figures, or whose invention produces
wonderful harmonic combination, can or ought to
force upon a symphonic theme the same numerous,
delicate and varied poetical changes which the motives in a music drama naturally assume. The Rhine-
daughter Motive, for instance, after expressing every
passion which is awakened by the ever changing action of a drama, appears in the first act of the "Götterdämmerung " in a form which seems to me utterly
inconsistent with the purposes of a symphony. For,
although the motive in that peculiar phase seems to
owe its existence to harmonic and thematic laws
only, close inspection will show that the drama itself
required the application of these laws. To adapt in a
symphony what is found possible here would be at-

tended with most pernicious results ; for the effect which seems natural and logical in a music drama would in a symphony seem labored and unreasonable.

I do not care to repeat here all I have already said concerning music in its relation to the drama. I desired only to point out the differences in two applications of music, by a confusion of which one artistic form is ruined and the other misunderstood. And this seemed to me necessary to a full æsthetic understanding of the wonderful events in the development of music—the only art in which at the present time any healthy progress can be observed—whereas in regard to this very development there is now a most lamentable confusion of ideas. For in departing from symphonic laws, composers, when they approached the drama, never got farther than the opera, which only embarrassed the powers of the great symphonists. When we wonder at the infinite variety of forms created by similar powers when music is brought into proper communion with the drama, we must remember that these forms become blurred when transferred from the music drama to the symphony. As it would require too much space to follow up all these novel changes and their complicated relation, I close by pointing to the difference between the original form and modulations of the motive in a music drama and the salient points in the character and development of the symphonic theme.

Properly speaking, we can not conceive a principal symphonic theme with striking harmonic modulations ; especially if it appears at first in such a distracting outfit. The network of strange progressive harmonies with which the composer of "Lohengrin" closes the first arioso of "Elsa," who is entranced by the remembrance of a dream, would seem strained and unintelligible in the andante of a symphony; whereas in my music drama it is so logical and natural that I have never heard complaints to the contrary. This has its reason in the scenic action: *Elsa* steps forward in gentle sorrow, slowly and with modestly inclined countenance; only one musing glance interrupts her reverie. Her only answer is the relation of the dream which promises her relief; her glance had already told this, and now, looking boldly from the vision to the realization of its promises, she exclaims: "I will await his coming; he shall my champion be!" Then the musical phrase returns, after numerous digressions, to the original key. A young friend, to whom I sent the score for piano arrangement, was astonished at the many modulations to which this phrase was subjected in so few bars. But he was more astonished to find these changes perfectly natural at the first performance of "Lohengrin" at Weimar under Liszt, who had changed the optical spectre to a well formed tone figure.

It seems to me that there is a great deal in my works against which "professors" protest which appears quite simple to the majority of unprejudiced listeners. Should they place me in their chairs they would probably be dumbfounded at the moderation in the use of harmonic effects I should recommend to their pupils. The first rule I should lay down would be: "Never leave a key so long as you can say what you have to say—in that key." If this rule were followed, we might expect to hear symphonies worthy of comment, instead of our latest symphonies, which are beneath notice.

For that reason I now remain silent, until I am called to a conservatory—but not as "professor."

FROM THE "MUSIC OF THE FUTURE."

In Italy, where the opera was first elaborated, no other task has ever been set before the musician than to write a number of airs for special singers, in whom dramatic talent was entirely a secondary consideration —airs that should give these virtuosi an opportunity to bring into play their several specific vocal powers. All that poetry and scenery contributed to this exhibition of the performer's art was an excuse for time and space for it. With the singer alternated the dancer, who danced precisely the same as the other sang ; and the composer had no other task than to contribute variations on a certain selected type of tune.

* * * * * * *

For the German musician who looked out from his own field of choral and instrumental music upon that of dramatic music there existed no complete and attractive form in the line of opera which, by its relative perfection, could serve him as an example in such a way as he could be served in those classes of music which were more in his own school. While a noble, completed form of composition lay before him in the oratorio, and especially in the symphony, the opera merely offered him a disconnected chaos of trifling and undeveloped methods, upon which there rested the burden of a conventionality incomprehensible to him and subversive of all efforts towards free development.

*   *   *   *   *   *   *

It is said that Rossini once asked his teacher if it was necessary to learn counterpoint in order to compose an opera ? And as the latter, having in mind the modern Italian opera, replied that it was not, his pupil gladly abandoned it. After my teacher had taught me the most difficult portions of counterpoint he said to me : " Probably you will never have occasion to write a fugue ; but the fact that you can write one will give you technical independence and make everything else easy to you."

*   *   *   *   *   *   *

Having at hand the opinions of the greatest critics —the investigations, for instance, of a Lessing into the limits of painting and poetry—I believed that I might form the theory that every individual branch of art follows out a development of its powers that finally leads it to their limits, and that it cannot pass these limits without the danger of losing itself in the unintelligible and absolutely fantastic, even in the absurd. I thought that I saw in this point the necessity for it to join companionship at this stage with another class of art, related to it, and the only one capable of going on from this position.

*   *   *   *   *   *   *

The conflict between the adherents of Gluck and those of Piccini, in Paris, was nothing but a contro-

versy (from its very nature indecisive) on the question whether the ideal of the drama was attainable
through the opera. Those who believed they could
sustain successfuily the affirmative side of this question were, in spite of their apparent victories, held in
serious check by their opponents as soon as these
latter treated music as predominating in opera to
such an extent that the result was to be attributed to
it and not to poetry. Voltaire, who in the abstract
inclined to the affirmative opinion, saw himself forced,
as far as the concrete state of the case was concerned, to the condemnatory remark: "Ce qui est
trop sot pour être dit on le chante"—(what is too
stupid to be spoken is sung).

Let us establish first of all the fact that the one true
form of music is melody ; that without melody music
is inconceivable, and that music and melody are insep-
arable.

That a piece of music has no melody can, therefore, only mean that the musician has not attained
to the real formation of an effective form that can
have a decisive influence upon the feelings, which
simply shows the absence of talent in the composer,
his want of originality compelling him to make up his
piece from hackneyed melodic phrases to which the
ear is utterly indifferent. But in the mouth of the
uncultured frequenter of the opera, and when used
with regard to real music, the expression of this opinion betrays the fact that only a fixed and narrow form
of melody is meant, such as (as we have already seen)
belongs to a very childish stage of musical art; and

for this reason an exclusive liking for such a form must also seem childish to us.

* * * * * * *

The great melody I have in mind should produce an effect upon one's spirits like that which a beautiful forest produces in a summer evening upon a lonely wanderer who has but just left the town. The peculiarity of this impression, which I leave to the experienced reader to trace out in all its effects upon the soul, is the appreciation of a silence that grows more and more eloquent with every moment. It is enough for the objects of a work of art, generally speaking, if it has produced this fundamental impression, and can by its means sway the listener and bring him still further into a mood of higher purpose ; unconsciously he begins to share its elevating tendency. But the wanderer in the wood, when, overcome by the general impression, he is fairly established in the lasting mood that follows it, develops his mental powers into new capabilities of perception, listens ever more keenly, as one who hears with new senses and becomes with every moment more distinctly conscious of endlessly varied voices that are abroad in the forest. New and various ones constantly join, such as he never remembers to have heard before, and as they multiply in numbers they increase in mysterious power. They grow louder and louder, and so many are the voices, the separate tunes he hears, that the whole, strong, clear swelling music seems to him again only the great forest melody that enchained

him with awe at the beginning, just as the deep blue
heaven at night had riveted his gaze, which, the
longer it remained absorbed in the spectacle, saw
more distinctly, clearly and brightly its countless
hosts of stars. This melody will forever echo within
him, yet he cannot hum it over to himself, and to hear
it again he must go again into the woods on a summer
evening as before. How foolish would he be if he
sought to catch one of these bright forest songsters,
to carry it home with him that it might whistle for
him some little part of that great forest melody.
What else would he hear, if he did so, but simply a
bit of melody, after all ?

FROM "OPERATIC POETRY AND COMPOSITION."

I have frequently noticed during my long experience that many who visit the opera pay little heed to
the plot or action which the music is supposed to represent. This is not, perhaps, a matter for regret in such
operas as "Don Juan" or "Nozze de Figaro," because, as long as the embarrassing situations remain
unintelligible to youthful hearers, the music of these
operas can always form parts of a course of study
without corrupting the morals of the student. It is
quite fortunate that the plot of "Robert le Diable"
and "The Huguenots" can be understood only by the
initiated ; but I was surprised to hear the other day
that even "The Freischütz" remained a mystery to
many until I became conscious that I myself did not
perfectly recollect some of the parts, even though I

had conducted the opera time and again. My friends first blamed our singers and then began to abuse their pronunciation, when I called their attention to the fact that many operas contain a good deal of spoken dialogue. This frequently keeps German audiences in total ignorance of plot and action—an ignorance, however, which I believe many composers share with them. In France people require a fine *pièce;* the libretto must be amusing, even without the music, except perhaps in the grand opera, where a good ballet condones for the greatest insipidity.

*   *   *   *   *   *   *

The librettos of Italian operas are very trifling, since in Italy operas are composed not according to the requirements of good music, but of bravura singers. Yet even Italian operas, although they are all written according to one and the same pattern, are more enjoyable if the hearer has an idea of the plot and action. Not even this, however, can save Rossini's "Semiramide."

*   *   *   *   *   *   *

In "Nozze de Figaro" Mozart proves himself thoroughly conversant with the methods of his art. His work was so symmetrical that he was justified in refusing, even at the emperor's request, to allow a single note to be struck out of some parts of the opera. Into what would have been tedious recitative in Italian operas Mozart breathed life and soul. As in Beethoven's symphonies even a pause is eloquent, so in Mozart's opera everything is full of spirit and action, and the orchestral internezzos give full musical expression to the struggle between cunning and cool foresight on the one hand and passionate brutality on the other. The dialogue is music and the music is dialogue, something which Mozart could not have accomplished without a knowledge of instrumentation unheard of until then, and perhaps not even equaled in our own day.

* * * * * * *

A German prince, who thought he could compose operas, sent me word, through my friend Liszt, that he desired my aid in the orchestration of his work, and that he was particularly anxious to profit by the effective manner in which I employed the trombones in "Tannhäuser;" whereupon Liszt gave him the recipe by saying that I never scored before I had an idea.

* * * * * * *

Years ago the success of my operas at the Royal Theatre in Dresden attracted the attention of F. Hiller, and afterward of Robert Schumann, for both wondered how a composer who was hardly known could keep his works before the public. Finally they attributed my success to my librettos, and came to ask my aid in writing the text for operas of their own. This assistance they afterward declined, fearing, no doubt, I might play them some mean trick. Of "Lohengrin," Schumann said that it was unfit for musical accompaniment, though his opinion differed widely from that of Taubert in Berlin, who liked my libretto, and said, after he had heard my opera, that *he would like to write music of his own to my text.* No representations of mine could induce Schumann to eliminate the insipid third act from the libretto to " Genoveva." Yet no one seems disposed to censure such total disregard of artistic principles.

WAGNER'S CRITICS.

WAGNER'S CRITICS.

RICHARD WAGNER has been censured for his arrogance and his bitterness. Yet his critics were the first to open the sluices of invective. Were they not the men who, when Wagner was young and struggling for recognition, took advantage of their position as critics to cast every slur upon his efforts and to abuse his music as though he were committing a crime against the art and trying to throttle it outright ? Mendelssohn opened the war by declaring that Wagner was only a talented dilettante, and Schumann followed him when he said, speaking of "Tannhäuser:" "Wagner is, to tell the plain truth, not a good musician ; he lacks form and is wanting in ideas of euphony. * * * His music is hollow, disagreeable and often amateurish." After him other musicians and writers, belonging to Germany, France and England, continued to sharpen their wit on the music of the future. The *Echo*, a musical journal published in Berlin, called the tetralogy "Bayreuth cabbage." A Lyonese feuilletonist spoke of Wagner as the "méprisable Bavarois," and a London critic described his compositions as "weeds growing on the grave of Beethoven."

There is a very interesting book, published by Joh. André, in Offenbach, known as the "Richard Wagner Catalogue." In it Kastner and Tappert, admirers of the composer, have collected all that has been said or written concerning the object of their devotion in pamphlets, monographs, musical periodicals and daily journals. The work has been carried out faithfully, too faithfully perhaps in some respects, for it contains many remarks and aphorisms which can be but the growth of heated discussion or after dinner wit.

Musical criticism has increased during the present century, and its growth is perhaps greatly due to the animosity of Wagner's opponents who attacked his theories in the columns of the press, while he defended them not only by critical verbiage, but by the more practical method of illustration in his musical compositions. Wagner's animosity appears pardonable, his labors seem stupendous after a perusal of the volume issued by Messrs. Kastner and Tappert. He entered upon his career when custom fettered the thoughts of musicians and controlled the opinions of critics, who in turn dictated their system of musical ethics to the public. Wagner stood almost alone. Against him were arrayed technical forms sanctioned by long usage ; so-called composers, who pillaged the works of great predecessors, and hated him because they feared a reformer who despised and exposed them, and critics who thought that, having read all existing books on music, they could learn no more ; who forgot that genius never follows existing laws, but creates new laws of its own ; and who had taught audiences to regard established forms as indispensable to musical composition. As a result, Wagner met with more than passive resistance—with open warfare. His opponents were vindictive and bitter, and at first he met them almost single handed. Admiration for his courage, which seemed to grow as the opposition increased, kept him before the public, until he had gathered around him a sufficient number of supporters to achieve the brilliant triumph of Bayreuth.

The Wagner Catalogue furnishes a good many specimens of the deplorable condition of German and French musical criticism not so many years ago.

" Tannhäuser " seems to have troubled others quite as much as it did Mendelssohn and Schumann. *" Se tannhäuser "* (to be bored) was a verb in common use among the frequenters of the Paris boulevards. A parody on the opera was published in France, entitled *" Tanne-aux-airs,* par M. Vagnes-Nerfs," in which *Elizabeth* figures as *Elisa-bête.* Scudo says the overture is a badly constructed musical machine ; and Truhn, in the *Berliner Figaro* of 1873, calls the song to the evening star a cat serenade. In 1856 Dr. Eduard Schmidt called " Tannhäuser " " music of dissonances," and foretold its disappearance from the stage after two performances. During the same year another Berlin critic, Otto Lindner, exclaimed in the *Vossische Zeitung :* " What a difference between a talented man and a musician of the future ! "

Of the overture to "The Flying Dutchman " it was
said that it made one seasick to hear it ; the overture
to "Rienzi" is called circus music, in No. 34 of the
Echo for 1872, and the same paper exclaimed (No. 22,
1871): "Wagner's huge, tragic, bombastic ' Rienzi,' this
operatic monstrum ! the musical value of the score
equals zero and is far below the standard of Bellini."
In 1873 the *Echo* speaks of "the brassy opera ' Lohengrin,' a caricature of music."

E. Berusdart calls the "Faust Overture" hollow and
tedious. "The Meistersinger," however, excited most
ridicule. On the 4th of April, 1870, the *Montags Zeitung*
of Berlin had the following squib : " The manager of
the Royal Opera has issued this manifesto : Since capital punishment has been abolished no one is obliged
to hear ' The Meistersinger' more than once." In November, 1875, the same paper remarked : " The Royal
Opera troupe will soon give ' The Meistersinger,' that
most terrible of terrible operas." An imaginary operatic manager, about to produce this work, asks : " Why
was I born in the same century with this fellow ? "
Ferdinand Hiller calls the riot scene in " The Meistersinger " "the most insane attempt to murder art,
taste, music and poetry."

"Tristan und Isolde" also came in for a good round
of abuse. Ed. Scheller remarked in 1865 : " The poem
is in every respect absurd ; the music, with the excep-
tion of a few numbers, is the refined brewing of a de-
bilitated and morbid imagination." The following also
should be quoted : " The introduction to ' Tristan und
Isolde ' is a chaos of sound. One would think a bomb

had exploded in the midst of a musical composition and scattered the notes." Heinrich Dorn calls the "Kaisermarsch" an insult to the Emperor of Germany.

Apropos of "Rhinegold," Hanslick wrote that the text was made up of bombastic, alliterative stammerings. It was also called, from the peculiar cries of the *Rhinedaughters*, "wigalaweia" music, and the scene in which the *Rhinedaughters* appear is called an "aquarium" by Wilhelm Mohr. "The composer of the 'Nibelungen' is an idle dreamer," said O. Triese, in 1874, and the tetralogy is characterized as "music stuffed with leading motives." In the *Echo* (No. 39, 1876), Speidel, writing of the same work, says: "Wagner, none of whose musical ideas are drawn from the depths of his nature, is a clever imitator of actual events ; his music is like an educated monkey."

In May, 1872, Speidel had written : "Richard Wagner's artistic career can no longer be separated from the artistic career of entire Germany. * * * Richard Wagner is undoubtedly the greatest operatic composer of our time. * * * Without regarding the merits or demerits of his work it can be said to possess some positive qualities : it creates enthusiasm—enthusiasm among the entire German nation—wherever it visits the opera. * * * The German nation sees in it the realization of its ideal ; and whoever tears away that ideal tears it out of the heart of the entire race." During the years from 1872 to 1876 there must have been a curious revolution in Mr. Speidel's ideas.

The following, from the *Berliner Montags Zeitung*, May 4, 1874, is a hit at " Die Walküre : "

" For the fair in support of the Wagner fund we have received :

" Cigar cases of burst drum skins.

" Piano arrangement of the score of the opera ' Cosima* Fan tutti,' by Hans v. Bülow.

" Ear wads for people who are going to the performances of the ' Walküre.' "

Albert Wagner, Richard's brother, said : " He can write poetry, but he can't compose."

Beside the criticisms applied to specific compositions, many offensive remarks were applied generally to the music of the future and its supporters.

These are a few instances :

" It is a well-known fact that 99 per cent. of Wagner's admirers are unmusical." (H. Truhn, April, 1872.)

" The so-called dramatic music of the Chinese is unmusical and declamatory, like the music of the future." (*Signale*, 1863.)

" Richard Wagner stretches the imagination with the same means as romancists and charlatans."

" Berlioz and Wagner are two *enfants terribles* of Beethoven."

No. 38 of the Vienna *Signale*, 1864, says : " Since Wagner has found a solid basis in Munich for wholesale operatic performances, there is a feeling of security in Vienna, because, no doubt, the next Wagner operas will explode in Munich."

---

* The name of Liszt's daughter, who married Von Bülow, was divorced from him and then married Wagner.

Joachim refused the invitation of the committee of the Vienna Beethoven Festival because Wagner also had been similarly requested to co-operate, whereupon the *Echo* remarks : " No one will doubt the privilege of private persons to avoid the society of suspicious characters ; in the case of an artist this right should be denied least of all."

" Moral seediness is the proper expression for the feeling engendered by hearing Wagner's music." (Dr. W. Mohr, 1872.)

Wagner's followers are called " a vulgar crowd " more than once, and Paul Heyse summed up the characteristics of his music in the words " pathetic cancan."

Wagner himself is called the great cacophonist ; a literary, poetical and musical humbug ; a Don Quixote ; a musical Münchausen ; the hangman of modern art ; the noisiest man of our century ; and finally, in terms of irony, Richard the Great, the infallible, the Divine, the Pope among musicians ! (*Signale*).

Numerous other specimens of the vituperations indulged in by Wagner's opponents might be quoted, but many are lengthy articles.

Wagner, like every true artist, strove for recognition—not of himself—but of the ideal he worshipped. He dictated to the public, and at first the public rebelled. Had he then made concessions he might have enjoyed immediate wealth and popularity. If he abandoned old forms it was not because he could not, but because he would not follow in the traditionary path. For he had laid down for his guidance during his artis-

tic career certain principles, and from these he never
swerved.   Opposition   only   strengthened   him   and
nerved him for the great struggle.   What he felt to be
true the public should acknowledge to be true, and to
this end he cast aside all hope of immediate success
and dedicated his life to the art he loved so well.   And
so he kept on his way.   The public wondered and
critics scoffed, then the public began to follow, at first
reluctantly, at last cheerfully—in spite of the fact that
critics continued to dredge their brains.

As before remarked, all that has been said, both by
friend and foe, is gathered in the volume of Messrs.
Kastner and Tappert, and the book forms for this reason an excellent review of the great musical struggle.

To the historian it is of incalculable value.   The
future writer who can look calmly and dispassionately
upon the heated discussions of our generation will perhaps smile superciliously at arguments which time has
taught him to regard as useless, and criticism which
in his day he will know to have been unavailing.   For
if it were possible to draw aside the curtain which
hides the future of the divine art, it would not be sur-
prising to find that, long after the captious critics of
the great reformer had been forgotten, Wagner's compositions were transmitted from generation to generation as enduring monuments of his fame, and should
some of his critics be remembered it would be only
because, though small hunters, they went gunning
after such big game.

WAGNER'S OPERAS.

ERICK.

18 63   Der fliegende Holländer.

WAGNER'S OPERAS.

"Rienzi" is based upon Bulwer's novel of the same title, the scene of the opera being laid in Rome toward the middle of the fourteenth century. *Orsini*, a Roman patrician, attempts to abduct *Irene*, the sister of *Rienzi*, a papal notary, but is opposed at the critical moment by *Colonna*, another patrician. A fight ensues between the two factions, in the midst of which *Adriano*, the son of *Colonna*, who is in love with *Irene*, appears to defend her. A crowd is attracted by the tumult, and among others *Rienzi* comes upon the scene. Enraged at the insult offered his sister, and stirred on by *Cardinal Raimondo*, he urges the people to resist the outrages of the nobles. *Adriano* is impelled by his love for *Irene* to cast his lot with her brother. The nobles are overpowered, and appear at the capitol to swear allegiance to *Rienzi*, but during the festal proceedings *Adriano* warns him that the nobles have plotted to kill him. An attempt which *Orsini* makes upon him with a dagger is frustrated by a steel breast plate which *Rienzi* wears under his robe.

The nobles are seized and condemned to death, but on *Adriano's* pleading they are spared. They, how-

ever, violate their oath of submission, and the people
again under *Rienzi's* leadership rise and exterminate
them, *Adriano* having pleaded in vain. But the popular tide turns against *Rienzi*, especially in consequence
of the report that he is in league with the German
emperor, and intends to restore the Roman pontiff to
power. As a festive procession is escorting *Rienzi* to
church *Adriano* rushes upon him with a drawn dagger,
being infuriated at the slaughter of his family, but the
blow is averted. Instead of the *Te Deum*, however,
with which *Rienzi* expected to be greeted on his entrance to the church he hears the malediction and
sees the ecclesiastical dignitaries placing the ban of
excommunication against him upon the doors. *Adriano* hurries to *Irene* to warn her of her brother's danger, and urges her to seek safety with him in flight.
She, however, repels him, and seeks her brother, determined to die with him, if need be. She finds him at
prayer in the capitol, but rejects his counsel to save
herself with *Adriano*. *Rienzi* appeals to the infuriated
populace which has gathered around the capitol, but
they do not heed him.   They fire the capitol with their
torches, and hurl stones at *Rienzi* and *Irene*.   As *Adriano* sees his beloved one and her brother doomed to
death in the flames, he throws away his sword, rushes
into the capitol and perishes with them.

The overture of " Rienzi " gives a vivid idea of the
action of the opera. Soon after the beginning there is
heard the broad and stately melody of *Rienzi's* prayer,
and then the Rienzi Motive, a typical phrase which is
used with great effect later in the opera.   It is the only

motive employed in the work, is not at all varied, and while interesting as showing the bent of Wagner's mind can hardly be said to foreshadow his masterly system of later invention. It is followed in the overture by the lively melody heard in the concluding portion of the finale of the second act. These are the three most conspicuous portions of the overture, in which there are, however, numerous tumultuous passages reflecting the dramatic excitement which pervades many scenes.

The opening of the first act is full of animation, the orchestra depicting the tumult which prevails during the struggle between the nobles. *Rienzi's* brief recitative is a masterpiece of declamatory-music, and his call to arms is spirited. It is followed by a trio between *Irene, Rienzi* and *Adriano,* and this in turn by a duet for the two last named which is full of fire. The finale opens with a double chorus for the populace and the monks in the Lateran, accompanied by the organ. Then there is a broad and energetic appeal to the people from *Rienzi,* and amid the shouts of the populace and the ringing tones of the trumpets the act closes.

The insurrection of the people against the nobles is successful, and *Rienzi,* in the second act, awaits at the capitol the patricians who are to pledge him their submission. The act opens with a broad and stately march, to which the messengers of peace enter. They sing a graceful chorus. This is followed by a chorus for the senators, and the nobles then tender their submission. There is a terzette between *Adriano, Colonna* and

Orsini, in which the nobles express their contempt for the young patrician. The finale which then begins is highly spectacular. There is a march for the embassadors, and a grand ballet, somewhat historical in character, and supposed to be symbolical of the triumphs of ancient Rome. In the midst of this occurs the assault upon *Rienzi*. *Rienzi's* pardon of the nobles is conveyed in a broadly beautiful melody, and this is succeeded by the animated passage heard in the overture. With it are mingled the chants of the monks, the shouts of the people who are opposed to the cardinal and nobles, and the tolling of bells.

The third act opens tumultuously. The people have been aroused by fresh outrages on the part of the nobles. *Rienzi's* emissaries disperse, after a furious chorus, to rouse the populace to vengeance. After they have left, *Adriano* has his great air, a number which can never fail of effect when sung with all the expression of which it is capable. The rest of the act is a grand accumulation of martial music or noise, whichever one chooses to call it, and includes the stupendous battle hymn, which is accompanied by the clashing of swords and shields, the ringing of bells, and all the tumult incidental to a riot. In this the Rienzi Motive is introduced with great effect. After *Adriano* has pleaded in vain with *Rienzi* for the nobles, and the various bands of armed citizens have dispersed, there is a duet between *Adriano* and *Irene*, in which *Adriano* takes farewell of her. The victorious populace appears, and the act closes with their triumphant shouts. The fourth act is brief, and, beyond the description given in the synopsis of the part, requires no further comment.

The fifth act opens with the beautiful prayer of *Rienzi*, already familiar from the overture. There is a tender duet between *Rienzi* and *Irene*, an impassioned aria for *Rienzi*, a duet for *Irene* and *Adriano*, and then the finale, which is chiefly choral.

"THE FLYING DUTCHMAN."

From " Rienzi " Wagner took a giant stride to " The Flying Dutchman." This is the first milestone on the road from the opera to the music drama. Of " Rienzi" the composer was in after years ashamed, writing to Liszt: "I, as an artist and man, have not the heart for the reconstruction of that, to my taste, superannuated work, which, in consequence of its immoderate dimensions, I have had to remodel more than once. I have no longer the heart for it, and desire from all my soul to do something new instead." He spoke of it as a youthful error, but in " The Flying Dutchman " there is little, if anything, which could have troubled his artistic conscience. One can hardly imagine the legend more effectively treated dramatically and musically than it is in Wagner's libretto and score. It is a work of wild and sombre beauty, relieved only occasionally by touches of light and grace, and has all the interest attaching to a work in which for the first time a genius feels himself conscious of his greatness. If it is not as impressive as "Tannhäuser " or " Lohengrin," nor as stupendous as the music dramas, that is because the subject of the work

is lighter. As his genius developed, his choice of subjects and his treatment of them passed through as
complete an evolution as his musical theory, so that
when he finally abandoned the operatic form and
adopted the system of the leading motives, he conceived as the dramatic basis of his scores dramas which
it would be difficult to fancy set to any other music
than that which is characteristic of his music dramas.

Wagner's libretto is based upon the weirdly picturesque legend of " The Flying Dutchman "—the Wan-
dering Jew of the ocean. A Dutch captain, who, we
are told, attempted to double the Cape of Good Hope
in the teeth of a furious gale, swore that he would accomplish his purpose even if he kept on sailing forever.
The devil, hearing the oath, condemned the captain to
sail the sea until the judgment day, without hope of
release, unless he could find a woman who would love
him faithfully unto death. Once in every seven years
he is allowed to go ashore in search of a woman who
will redeem him through her faithful love.

The opera opens just as a term of seven years has
elapsed. "The Flying Dutchman " comes to anchor
in a bay of the coast of Norway, in which the ship of
Daland, a Norwegian sea captain, has sought shelter
from the storm. *Daland's* home is not far from the
bay, and the *Dutchman*, learning he has a daughter,
asked permission to woo her, offering him in return
all his treasures. *Daland* readily consents. His daughter, *Senta*, is a romantic maiden, upon whom the legend of " The Flying Dutchman " has made a deep
impression. As *Daland* ushers the *Dutchman* into his

home, *Senta* is gazing dreamily upon a picture representing the unhappy hero of the legend. The resemblance of the stranger to the face in this picture is so
striking that the emotional girl is at once attracted to
him, and pledges him her faith, deeming it her mission
to save him. Later on, *Eric*, a young huntsman, who
is in love with her, pleads his cause with her, and the
Dutchman, overhearing them, and thinking himself
again forsaken, rushes off to his vessel. *Senta* cries
out that she is faithful to him, and endeavors to follow
him, but is held back by *Eric*, *Daland* and her friends.
The *Dutchman*, who really loves *Senta*, then proclaims
who he is, thinking to terrify her, and at once puts to
sea. But she, undismayed by his words, and truly
faithful unto death, breaks away from those who are
holding her, and rushing to the edge of a cliff casts
herself into the ocean, with her arms stretched out
toward him. The phantom ship sinks, the sea rises
high and falls back into a seething whirlpool. In the
sunset glow the forms of *Senta* and the *Dutchman* are
seen rising in each other's embrace from the sea and
floating upward.

In " The Flying Dutchman " Wagner employs several
leading motives, not, indeed, with the skill which he displays in his music dramas, but with considerably greater
freedom of treatment than in "Rienzi." There we
had but one leading motive, which never varied in
form. The overture, which may be said to be an eloquent and beautiful musical narrative of the whole
opera, contains all these leading motives. It opens
with a stormy passage, out of which there bursts the

strong but sombre Motive of the Flying Dutchman himself, the dark hero of the legend. The orchestra fairly seethes and rages like the sea roaring under the lash of a terrific storm. And through all this furious orchestration there is heard again and again the motive of the *Dutchman*, as if his figure could be seen amid all the gloom and fury of the elements. There he stands, hoping for death, yet indestructible. As the excited music gradually dies away, there is heard a calm, somewhat undulating phrase which occurs in the opera when the *Flying Dutchman's* vessel puts into the quiet Norwegian harbor. Then, also, there occurs again the motive of the *Dutchman*, but this time played softly, as if the storm driven wretch had at last found a moment's peace.

We at once recognize to whom it is due that he has found this moment of repose, for we hear like prophetic measures the strains of the beautiful ballad which is sung by *Senta* in the second act of the opera, in which she relates the legend of " The Flying Dutchman " and tells of his unhappy fate. She is the one whom he is to meet when he goes ashore. The entire ballad is not heard at this point, only the opening measures of it, and these may be taken as indicating in this overture the simplicity and beauty of *Senta's* character. In fact, it would not be too much to call this opening phrase the Senta Motive. It is followed again by the phrase which indicates the coming to anchor of the *Dutchman's* vessel; then we hear again the motive of the *Dutchman* himself, dying away with the faintest possible effect. With sudden energy the orchestra dashes into the surging ocean music again, introducing this time the wild, pathetic plaint sung by the *Dutchman* in the first act of the opera. Again we hear his motive, and again the music seems to represent the surging, swirling ocean when aroused by a furious tempest. Even when we hear the measures of the sailors' chorus the orchestra continues its furious pace, making it appear as if the sailors were shouting above the storm. Characteristic in this overture, and also throughout the opera, especially in *Senta's* ballad, is what may be called the Ocean Motive, which most graphically depicts the wild and terrible aspect of the ocean during a storm. It is varied from time to time, but never loses its characteristic force and weirdness. The overture ends with an impassioned burst of melody based upon a portion of the concluding phrases of *Senta's* ballad ; phrases which we hear again at the end of the opera when she sacrifices herself in order to save her lover.

A wild and stormy scene is disclosed when the curtain rises upon the first act. The sea occupies the greater part of the scene, and stretches itself out far toward the horizon. A storm is raging. *Daland's* ship has sought shelter in a little cove formed by the cliffs. Sailors are employed in furling sails and coiling ropes. *Daland* is standing on a rock, looking about him to discover in what place they are. The orchestra, chiefly with the wild ocean music heard in the overture, depicts the raging of the storm, and above it are heard the shouts of the sailors at work: " Ho-jo-he ! Hal-lo-jo ! " *Daland* discovers that they have missed their port by seven miles on account of **the storm,** and deplores his bad luck that when so near **his home** and his beloved child he should have been driven **out** of his course.   As the storm seems to be abating **the** sailors descend into the hold and *Daland* goes **down** into the cabin to rest, leaving his steersman in **charge** of the deck.   The steersman walks the deck once **or** twice and then sits down near the rudder, yawning, and then rousing himself as if sleep were coming over him.   As if to force himself to remain awake he intones a sailor song, an exquisite little melody, with a dash of the sea in its undulating measures.   He intones the second verse, but sleep overcomes him and the phrases become more and more detached, until he at last falls asleep.

The storm begins to rage again and it grows darker. Suddenly the ship of the *Flying Dutchman*, with blood red sails and black mast, looms up in the distance. She glides over the waves as if she did not feel the storm at all, and quickly enters the harbor over against the ship of the Norwegian ; then silently and without the least noise the spectral crew furl the sails.   The *Dutchman* goes on shore.

Here now occurs the weird, dramatic recitative and aria : " The term is passed, and once again are ended seven long years."   As he is leaning in brooding silence against a rock in the foreground, *Daland* comes out of the cabin and observes the strange ship.   He rouses the steersman, who begins singing again a phrase of his song, until *Daland* points out the strange ship to him, when he springs up and hails her through a speaking trumpet. *Daland*, however, perceives the *Dutchman* and going ashore questions him. It is then that the *Dutchman*, after relating a mariner's story of ill luck and disaster, asks *Daland* to take him to his home and allow him to woo his daughter, and offers him his treasures. At this point we have a graceful and pretty duet, *Daland* readily consenting that the *Dutchman* accompany him. The storm having subsided and the wind being fair the crews of the vessels hoist sail to leave the port, *Daland's* vessel disappearing just as the *Dutchman* goes on board his ship.

After an introduction in which we hear a portion of the steersman's song, and also that phrase which denotes the appearance of the *Dutchman's* vessel in the harbor, the curtain rises upon a room in *Daland's* house. On the walls are pictures of vessels, charts, and on the farther wall the portrait of a pale man with a dark beard. *Senta*, leaning back in an armchair, is absorbed in dreamy contemplation of the portrait. Her old nurse, *Mary*, and her young friends, are sitting in various parts of the room, spinning. Here we have that charming musical number famous all the musical world over, perhaps largely through Liszt's admirable piano arrangement of it, the spinning chorus. For graceful and engaging beauty it cannot be surpassed, and may be cited as a striking instance of Wagner's gift of melody, should anybody at this late day be foolish enough to require proof of his genius in this respect. The girls tease *Senta* for gazing so dreamily at the portrait of the *Flying*

Dutchman, and finally ask her if she will not sing his ballad.

This ballad is a masterpiece of composition, vocally and instrumentally, being melodious as well as descriptive. It begins with the storm music familiar from the overture, and with the weird measures of the Flying Dutchman's Motive, which sound like a voice calling in distress from across the sea.

Senta repeats the measures of this motive, and then we have the simple and effective phrases beginning, " A ship the restless sweeps." Throughout this portion of the ballad the orchestra depicts the surging and heaving of the ocean, *Senta's* voice ringing out dramatically above the accompaniment. She then tells how he can be delivered from his curse, this portion being set to the measures which were heard in the overture, *Senta* finally proclaiming in the rapturous phrases with which the overture concluded that she is the woman who will save him by being faithful to him unto death. The girls about her spring up in terror and *Eric*, who has just entered the door and heard her outcry, hastens to her side. He brings news of the arrival of the vessel, and *Mary* and the girls hasten forth to meet the sailors. *Senta* wishes to follow, but *Eric* restrains her and pleads his love for her in melodious measures. *Senta*, however, will not give him an answer at this time. He then tells her of a dream he had, in which he saw a weird vessel from which two men, one her father, the other a ghastly looking stranger, made their way.

Her he saw going to the stranger and entreating him for his regard.

Senta, worked up to the highest pitch of excitement by *Eric's* words, now exclaims : "He seeks for me and I for him," and *Eric*, full of despair and horror, rushes away. *Senta*, after her outburst of excitement, remains again sunk in contemplation of the picture, softly repeating the measures of her romance. The door opens and the *Dutchman* and *Daland* appear. The *Dutchman* is the first to enter. *Senta* turns from the picture to him, and, uttering a loud cry of astonishment, remains standing as if transfixed without removing her eyes from the *Dutchman*. *Daland*, seeing that she does not greet him, comes up to her. She seizes his hand and after a hasty greeting asks him who the stranger is. *Daland* tells her, in measures of whose simple grace and beauty Mozart himself need not have been ashamed, of the stranger's request, and then leaves them alone. Then follows the duet, with its broad, smoothly flowing melody and its many phrases of dramatic power, in which *Senta* gives herself up unreservedly to the hero of her romantic attachment, *Daland* finally entering and adding his congratulations to their betrothal. This scene closes the act.

The music of it re-echoes through the introduction of the next act and goes over into a vigorous sailors' chorus and dance. The scene shows a bay with a rocky shore. *Daland's* house is in the foreground on one side, the background is occupied by his and the *Dutchman's* ship, which lie near one another. The

Norwegian ship is lighted up, and all the sailors are making merry on the deck. In strange contrast is the *Flying Dutchman's* vessel. An unnatural darkness hangs over it, and the stillness of death reigns aboard. The sailors and the girls in their merrymaking call loudly toward the Dutch ship to join them, but no reply is heard from the weird vessel. Finally the sailors call louder and louder and taunt the crew of the other ship. Then suddenly the sea, which has been quite calm, begins to rise. The storm wind whistles through the cordage of the "Flying Dutchman," and as dark bluish flames flare up in the rigging the weird crew show themselves, and sing a wild chorus, which strikes terror into all the merrymakers. The girls have fled, and the Norwegian sailors quit their deck, making the sign of the cross. The crew of the "Flying Dutchman" observing this, disappear with shrill laughter. Over their ship comes the stillness of death. Thick darkness is spread over it and the air and the sea become calm as before.

Senta now comes with trembling steps out of the house, followed by *Eric*. He pleads with her and entreats her to remember his love for her, and speaks also of the encouragement which she once gave him. The *Dutchman* has entered unperceived and has been listening. *Eric*, seeing him, at once recognizes the man of ghastly mien whom he saw in his vision. When the *Flying Dutchman* bids her farewell, because he deems himself abandoned, and *Senta* endeavors to follow him, *Eric* holds her and summons others to his aid. But, in spite of all resistance, *Senta* seeks to tear herself loose. Then it is that the *Flying Dutch-man* proclaims who he is and puts to sea. *Senta*, however, freeing herself, rushes to a cliff overhanging the sea, and calling out

> Praise thou thine angel for what he saith ;
> Here stand I faithful, yea, to death,

casts herself into the sea. Then occurs the conclud-ing tableau, the work ending with the portion of the ballad which brought the overture and spinning scene to a close.

" TANNHÄUSER."

The scene of " Tannhäuser " is laid at and near the Wartburg, where, during the thirteenth century, the Landgraves of the Thuringian Valley held sway. They were lovers of art, especially of poetry and music, and at the Wartburg many peaceful contests between the famous Minnesingers took place. Near this castle rises the Venusberg. According to tradition the in-terior of this mountain was inhabited by Holda, the Goddess of Spring, who, however, in time became identified with the Goddess of Love. Her court was filled with nymphs and sirens, and it was her greatest joy to entice into the mountain the knights of the Wartburg and hold them captive to her beauty. Among those whom she has thus lured into the rosy recesses of the Venusberg is *Tannhäuser*. In spite of her beauty, however, he is weary of her charms and longs again for a glimpse of the world. He seems to have heard the tolling of bells and other earthly sounds, and these stimulate his yearning to be set free from the magic charms of the goddess.

In vain she prophesies evil to him should he return to the world, and calling out that his hope rests in the Virgin he tears himself away from her. The court of *Venus* disappears and in a moment we see *Tannhäuser* lying before a cross in a valley upon which the Wartburg peacefully looks down. Pilgrims on their way to Rome pass him by and *Tannhäuser* thinks of joining them in order that he may obtain forgiveness for his crime in allowing himself to be enticed into the Venusberg. But the *Landgrave* and a number of his Minnesingers on their return from the chase come upon him and recognizing him endeavor to persuade him to return to the Wartburg with them, but vainly, until one of them, *Wolfram von Eschenbach*, tells him that since he has left the Wartburg a great sadness has come over the niece of the *Landgrave, Elizabeth*. It is evident that *Tannhäuser* has been in love with her, and that it is because of her beauty and virtue that he regrets so deeply having been lured into the Venusberg.

The *Landgrave*, feeling sure that *Tannhäuser* will win the prize at the contest of song soon to be held, offers the hand of his niece to the winner. The subject of the prize singing is love. The Minnesingers sing of the beauty of virtuous love, but *Tannhäuser*, suddenly remembering the seductive and magical beauties of the Venusberg, cannot control himself, and bursts out into a reckless hymn in praise of *Venus*. Horrified at his words, the knights draw their swords

TANNHÄUSER.

and would slay him but that *Elizabeth* throws herself between him and them. Crushed and penitent, *Tannhäuser* stands behind her, and the *Landgrave*, moved by her willingness to sacrifice herself for her sinful lover, announces that he will be allowed to join a second band of pilgrims who are going to Rome and to plead with the Pope for forgiveness.

Elizabeth prayerfully awaits his return ; but, as she is kneeling by the crucifix in front of the Wartburg, the pilgrims pass her by and in the band she does not see her lover. Slowly and sadly she returns to the castle to die. When the pilgrims' voices have died away, and *Elizabeth* has returned to the castle, leaving only *Wolfram*, who is also deeply enamored of her, upon the scene, *Tannhäuser* appears, weary and dejected. He has sought to obtain forgiveness in vain. The Pope had condemned him forever, proclaiming that no more than that his staff could put forth leaves could he expect forgiveness. He has come back to return again to the Venusberg. *Wolfram* seeks to retain him, but it is not until he mentions the name of *Elizabeth* that *Tannhäuser* is saved. A cortége approaches, and, as *Tannhäuser* recognizes the form of *Elizabeth* on the bier, he sinks down on her coffin and dies. Just then the second band of pilgrims arrive, bearing *Tannhäuser's* staff, which has put forth blossoms, thus showing that his sins have been forgiven.

From "The Flying Dutchman" to "Tannhäuser," dramatically and musically, is, if anything, a greater stride than from "Rienzi" to "The Flying Dutchman." In each of his successive works Wagner de-

monstrates greater and deeper powers as a dramatic
poet and composer. True it is that in nearly every
one of them woman appears as the redeeming angel
of sinful man, but the circumstances differ so that
this beautiful tribute always interests us anew. The
overture of the opera has long been a favorite piece
on concert programs. Like that of " The Flying
Dutchman " it is the story of the whole opera told in
music. It is certainly one of the most brilliant and
powerful pieces of orchestral music and its popularity
is easily understood. It opens with the melody of
the pilgrims' chorus, beginning softly as if coming
from a distance and gradually increasing in power
until it is heard in all its grandeur. At this point it
is joined by a violently agitated accompaniment on the
violins. This passage evoked great criticism when it
was first produced and for many years thereafter. It
was thought to mar the powerful beauty of the pilgrims' chorus. But without doing so at all it conveys
additional dramatic meaning, for these agitated
phrases depict the restlessness of the world as compared with the grateful tranquillity of religious faith
as set forth in the melody of the pilgrims' chorus.

Having reached a climax this chorus gradually dies
away, and suddenly, and with intense dramatic contrast,
we have all the seductive spells of the Venusberg
displayed before us—that is, musically displayed ; but
then the music is so wonderfully vivid, it depicts with
such marvelous clearness the many colored alluring
scene at the court of this unholy goddess, it gives
vent so freely to the sinful excitement which pervades

the Venusberg, that we actually seem to see what we hear. This passes over in turn to the outburst of passion in which *Tannhäuser* sings *Venus'* praise, and immediately after we have the boisterous and vigorous music which accompanies the threatening action of the *Landgrave* and Minnesingers when they draw their swords upon *Tannhäuser* in order to take vengeance upon him for his crimes. Upon these three episodes of the drama, which so characteristically give insight into its plot and action, the overture is based, and it very naturally concludes with the pilgrims' chorus, which seems to voice the final forgiveness of *Tannhäuser*.

The curtain then rises, disclosing all the seductive spells of the Venusberg. *Tannhäuser* lies in the arms of *Venus*, who reclines upon a flowery couch. Nymphs, sirens and satyrs are dancing about them and in the distance are grottoes alive with amorous figures. Various mythological amours, such as that of Leda and the swan, are supposed to be in progress, but fortunately at a mitigating distance. Much of the music familiar from the overture is heard during this scene, but it gains in effect from the distant voices of the sirens and, of course, by artistic scenery and grouping and well executed dances of the denizens of *Venus'* court. Very dramatic, too, is the scene between *Venus* and *Tannhäuser*, when the latter sings his hymn in her praise, but at the same time proclaims that he desires to return to the world. In alluring strains she endeavors to tempt him to remain with her, but when she discovers that he is bound

upon going she vehemently warns him of the misfortunes which await him upon earth and prophesies
that he will some day return to her and penitently
ask to be taken back into her realm.

Dramatic and effective as this scene is in the original score, it has gained immensely in power by the
additions which Wagner made for the productions in
Paris.   The overture does not, in this version, come
to a formal close, but, after the manner of Wagner's
later works, the transition is made directly from it to
the scene of the Venusberg.   The dances have been
elaborated and laid out upon a more careful allegorical basis and the music of *Venus* has been greatly
strengthened from a dramatic point of view, so that
now the scene in which she pleads him to remain and
afterward warns him against the sorrows to which he
will be exposed are among the finest of Wagner's
compositions, rivaling in dramatic power the ripest
work in his music dramas.

Wagner's knowledge of the stage is shown in the
wonderfully dramatic effect in the change of scene
from the Venusberg to the landscape in the valley of
the Wartburg.   One moment we have the many colored glory of the court of the Goddess of Love, with
all its dancing nymphs, sirens and satyrs, its beautiful
grottoes and alluring groups ; the next all this has
disappeared, and from the heated atmosphere of
Venus' unholy rites we are suddenly transported to a
peaceful scene whose influence upon us is deepened
by the crucifix in the foreground before which *Tannhäuser* kneels in penitence.   The peacefulness of the

VENUS.

scene is greatly enhanced by the appearance upon a rocky eminence to the left of a young shepherd who pipes a pastoral strain, while in the background are heard the tinkling of bells, as though his sheep were there grazing upon some upland meadow. Before he has finished piping his lay the voices of the pilgrims are heard in the distance, their solemn measures being interrupted by little phrases piped by the *Shepherd*. As the pilgrims approach, the chorus becomes louder, and as they pass over the stage and bow before the crucifix, their praise swells into an eloquent psalm of devotion.

Tannhäuser is deeply affected and gives way to his feelings in a deep lament, against which are heard the voices of the pilgrims as they recede in the distance. This whole scene is one of marvelous beauty, the contrast between it and the preceding scene being enhanced by the religiously tranquil nature of the episodes it introduces and the music which accompanies them. Upon the peaceful scene the notes of hunting horns now break in, and gradually the *Landgrave* and his hunters gather about *Tannhäuser*. *Wolfram* recognizes him and tells the others who he is. They greet him in an expressive septette, and *Wolfram*, finding he is bent upon following the pilgrims to Rome, asks permission of the *Landgrave* to inform him of the impression which he seems to have made upon *Elizabeth*. This he does in a melodious solo, and *Tannhäuser*, overcome by his love for *Elizabeth*, consents to return to the halls which have missed him so long. Exclamations of joy greet his decision, and the act closes with an enthusiastic ensemble, which is a glorious piece of concerted music and never fails of brilliant effect when it is well executed, especially if the representative *Tannhäuser* has enough voice left to make himself heard above the others, which has not been the case with some of the veterans of Wagnerian campaigns who have been heard here. The accompanying scenic grouping must also be in keeping with the composer's purpose. The *Landgrave's* suite should gradually arrive, bearing the game which has been slain, and hunting hounds should be led on the stage. Finally the *Landgrave* and Minnesingers mount horses and ride away toward the castle.

The scene of the second act is laid in the singers' hall of the Wartburg. The introduction depicts *Elizabeth's* joy at *Tannhäuser's* return, and when the curtain rises she at once enters and joyfully greets the scenes of *Tannhäuser's* former triumphs in broadly expressive dramatic phrases, which, although they may not form a melody from the old point of view, may be said to be more dramatically melodious than a melody. At all, events they are eloquent with joy. *Wolfram* then appears, conducting *Tannhäuser* to her. *Elizabeth* seems overjoyed to see him, but then checks herself, and her maidenly modesty, which veils her transport at meeting him, again finds expression in a number of hesitating but exceedingly beautiful phrases. She asks *Tannhäuser* where he has been, but he, of course, gives misleading answers. Finally, however, when he tells her she is the one who has attracted him back to the castle, their love finds expression in a swift and rapidly flowing dramatic duet, which unfortunately is rarely given in its entirety, although as a glorious outburst of emotional music it certainly deserves to be heard in the exact form and length in which the composer wrote it.

There is then a scene of much tender feeling between the *Landgrave* and *Elizabeth*, in which the former tells her that he will offer her hand as prize to the singer whom she shall crown as winner. The first strains of the grand march are then heard. This is one of Wagner's most brilliant and effective orchestral and vocal pieces. Though in perfect march rhythm it is not intended that the guests who assemble at the Wartburg shall enter like a company of soldiers. On the contrary, they arrive in irregular detachments, stride across the floor, and make their obeisance in a perfectly natural manner. After an address by the *Landgrave*, which can hardly be called remarkably interesting, the singers draw lots to decide who among them shall begin. This prize singing, while it is of intense dramatic interest, is unfortunately of not so great musical value as the rest of the score, and hence this scene somewhat mars the effect of the act. In fact, unless a person is sufficiently German to understand every word that is sung, and to be in complete sympathy with the legend, it is decidedly tedious. What, however, redeems it from failure is a gradually growing dramatic excitement, as *Tannhäuser* places himself in opposition to the Minnesingers, an excitement which reaches its climax when, no longer able to restrain himself, he bursts forth into his hymn in praise of the unholy charms of *Venus*.

The women shout in horror and rush from the hall as if the very atmosphere were tainted by his presence, and the men, drawing their swords, rush upon him. This brings us to the great dramatic moment, when, with a shriek, *Elizabeth*, whom he has cruelly wronged, throws herself protectingly before him, and thus appears a second time as his saving angel. In short and excited phrases the men pour forth their wrath at *Tannhäuser's* crime, and he, realizing its enormity, seems crushed with a consciousness of his guilt. Of wondrous beauty is the septette, " An angel has from heaven descended," which rises to a magnificent climax and is one of the finest pieces of dramatic writing in Wagner's scores, although, of course, it is really difficult to praise any of Wagner's music at the expense of anything else he has written, or to compare any one of his scores with another, for, except in few instances, he always rises to his dramatic opportunity. The voices of young pilgrims are heard in the valley, and the *Landgrave* then announces the conditions upon which *Tannhäuser* can again obtain admission to the Minnesingers' circle at the Wartburg, and *Tannhäuser* joins the pilgrims on their way to Rome.

The third act displays once more the valley of the Wartburg, the same scene as that to which the Venusberg changed in the first act. *Elizabeth*, arrayed in white, is kneeling, in deep prayer, before the crucifix. At one side, and watching her tenderly, stands *Wol-*

fram. After a sad recitative from *Wolfram*, the chorus of the returning pilgrims is heard in the distance. They sing the melody heard in the overture, and the same effect of gradual approach is produced by a magnificent crescendo as they reach and cross the scene. With almost piteous anxiety and grief *Elizabeth* scans them closely as they go by, to see if *Tannhäuser* be among them, and when the last one has passed and she realizes that he has not returned she sinks again upon her knees before the crucifix and sings the prayer, "Almighty Virgin, hear my sorrow," in whose music there is most beautifully combined the expression of poignant grief with trust in the will of the Almighty. As she rises and turns toward the castle, *Wolfram*, by his gesture, seems to ask her if he cannot accompany her, but she declines his offer and slowly goes her way up the mountain.

Meanwhile night has fallen upon the scene and the evening star glimmers softly above the castle. It is then that *Wolfram*, accompanying himself on the harp, intones the wondrously tender and beautiful song to the evening star, confessing therein his love for the saintly *Elizabeth*. Then *Tannhäuser*, dejected, footsore and weary, appears and in broken accents asks *Wolfram* to show him the way back to the Venusberg. *Wolfram* bids him stay his steps and persuades him to tell him the story of his pilgrimage. In fierce, dramatic accents *Tannhäuser* relates all that he has suffered on his way to Rome and the terrible judgment pronounced upon him by the Pope. This is a highly impressive episode, clearly foreshadowing Wagner's dramatic use of musical recitation in his later music dramas, and only an artist of the highest rank can do justice to it.

Tannhäuser proclaims that, having lost all chance of salvation, he will once more give himself up to the delights of the Venusberg. A roseate light illumines the recesses of the mountain and the unholy company of the Venusberg are again seen, *Venus* stretching out her arms for *Tannhäuser*, to welcome him. *Wolfram* struggles with the unhappy minstrel, and at last, when *Tannhäuser* seems unable to resist *Venus'* enticing voice any longer, *Wolfram* conjures him by the memory of *Elizabeth*. Then *Venus* knows that all is lost. The light dies away and the magic charms of the Venusberg disappear. Amid tolling of bells and mournful voices a funeral procession comes down the mountain. Recognizing the features of *Elizabeth*, the dying *Tannhäuser* falls upon her corpse. The younger pilgrims arrive with the staff, which has again put forth leaves, and amid the hallelujahs of the pilgrims the opera closes.

Beside the character of *Elizabeth* that of *Wolfram* stands out for its tender, manly beauty. In love with *Elizabeth*, he is yet the means of bringing back her lover to her, and in the end saves that lover from perdition, so that they may be united in death.

"LOHENGRIN."

"Lohengrin" differs entirely in character from "Tannhäuser," the contrast being so great as to form an admirable example of Wagner's extraordinary ver-

LOHENGRIN.

satility. The fact is that Wagner appears to have become so saturated with the subject of his dramas that he seems to have transported himself to the very time in which his scenes are laid. So vividly does he portray the mythological occurrences told in " Lohengrin " that one can almost imagine he had been an eye witness of them. This capacity of artistic reproduction of a remote period would alone entitle him to rank as a great dramatist. But he has done much more ; he has taken unpromising material, which to a writer of ordinary talent would be nothing at all, and converted it into a swiftly moving drama.

The material for " Lohengrin " was almost entirely lyric, but Wagner has made a stirring drama of it. Owing, however, to the character of the original, it is, while not at all lacking in strong dramatic situations, considerably more lyrical than " Tannhäuser." Consequently there is the same difference between the music of the two works, the harmonies of " Lohengrin " being more subtle and its melodiousness more subdued. It is, if anything, of a higher order than " Tannhäuser," and has, I believe, proved itself abroad to be the most popular of all his works, its popularity extending even to Italy. The music clothes the drama most admirably. The prelude at once places us in a proper mood for the story that is to unfold itself. It is based entirely upon one motive, and that a most beautiful one. Violins and flutes having with the most delicate intonation held long drawn out, ethereal chords, we hear on the violins, so divided as to heighten the delicacy of the effect, a motive which is intended to portray the sacred character of the Grail, the cup in which the Saviour's blood is supposed to have been caught as it flowed from the wound in His side while He was on the Cross.

Lohengrin is one of the knights of the Holy Grail who guard the sacred vessel. Although this motive alone occurs in the prelude, it never becomes monotonous, on account of the wonderful skill with which it is handled ; not that it is changed in form very frequently, but it works up through a magnificent crescendo to a tremendous climax with all the splendor of Wagner's instrumentation, to die away again to the ethereal whispers with which it began.

The story of " Lohengrin " is briefly as follows : The Hungarians have invaded Germany, and *Henry I.*, king of the Fatherland, visits Antwerp for the purpose of raising a force to combat them. He finds the country in a condition of anarchy. The dukedom is claimed by *Frederick*, who has married *Ortrud*, a daughter of the Prince of Friesland. The legitimate heir, *Gottfried*, has mysteriously disappeared, and his sister, *Elsa*, is charged by *Frederick* and *Ortrud* with having done away with him in order that she might obtain the sovereignty. The *King* summons her before him in order that the cause may be tried by the ordeal of single combat between *Frederick* and a champion who might be willing to appear for *Elsa*. None of the knights will defend her cause. She then describes a champion whose form has appeared to her in a vision, and she proclaims that he shall be her champion. Her pretense is derided by *Frederick* and his followers, who think that she is out of her mind, but after a triple summons by the *Herald* there is seen in the distance, on the river, a boat drawn by a swan, and in it a knight clad in silver armor. He comes to champion *Elsa's* cause, and before the combat betroths himself to her, but makes a strict condition that she shall never question him as to his name or birthplace, for if she should he would be obliged to return. She assents to the conditions, and the combat which ensues results in *Frederick's* ignominious defeat, and judgment of exile is pronounced on him.

Instead, however, of leaving the country he lingers in the neighborhood of Brabant, plotting with *Ortrud* how they may compass the ruin of *Lohengrin* and *Elsa*. *Ortrud* by her entreaties moves *Elsa* to pity, and persuades her to seek a reprieve for *Frederick*, at the same time, however, using every opportunity to instil doubts in *Elsa's* mind regarding her champion, and rousing her to such a pitch of nervous curiosity that she is on the point of asking him the forbidden question. After the bridal ceremonies, and in the bridal chamber, the distrust which *Ortrud* and *Frederick* have engendered in *Elsa's* mind so overcome her faith that she vehemently puts the forbidden question to her champion. Almost at the same moment *Frederick* and four of his followers force their way into the apartment, intending to take the knight's life. A single blow of *Lohengrin's* sword, however, stretches *Frederick* lifeless, and his followers bear his corpse away. Placing *Elsa* in the charge of her ladies in waiting, and ordering them to take her to the presence of the *King*, he repairs thither **him-self.**

The Brabantian hosts are gathering, and he is ex-pected to lead them to battle, but owing to *Elsa's* questions he is now obliged to disclose who he is and to take his departure. He proclaims that he is *Lohengrin*, son of *Parsifal*, Knight of the Holy Grail, and that he can linger no longer in Brabant, but must return to the place of his coming. The swan has once more appeared, drawing the boat down the river, and bidding *Elsa* farewell he steps into the little shell-like craft. But *Ortrud*, with malicious delight, declares that the swan is none other than *Elsa's* brother, whom she (*Ortrud*) bewitched into this form, and that he would have been changed back again to his human shape had it not been for *Elsa's* rashness. But *Lohengrin*, through his supernatural powers, is able to undo *Ortrud's* work, and at a word from him the swan disappears and *Gottfried* stands in its place. A dove now descends, and, hovering in front of the boat, draws it away with *Lohengrin*, while *Elsa* ex-pires in her brother's arms.

The first scene of the first act opens with a vigor-ous syncopated phrase, during which the curtain rises, disclosing a meadow on the banks of the Scheldt. Under a huge oak sits *King Henry*, surrounded by the counts and nobles of Saxony. Opposite to them stand nobles of Brabant; at their front *Frederick*, with *Ortrud* by his side. The *Herald* steps from the party of the *King* to the centre of the stage, and after a vigorous call from four trumpets on the stage, summons the princes, nobles and freemen of Brabant to muster to the realm's defense. During this scene *Frederick* arraigns *Elsa* and the summons for her to appear is issued. While there is no melody, properly speaking, in this scene, it is strongly effective, the four trumpets on the stage, with their characteristic calls, adding greatly to the force and dignity of the music. Then, too, *Frederick's* excitement and the short passages for the chorus greatly heighten the dramatic action. At the very close of the scene the *Herald's* summons to *Elsa* resounds. Immediately a change comes over the music, for *Elsa* enters, remaining some time at the back of the stage, then coming slowly and very timidly forward, the ladies of her train remaining during the first part of the scene in the extreme background. Clad in white, she appears so lovely and innocent that the men look upon her and softly whisper their surprise at the charge.

Most beautiful is the accompaniment of this scene —soft and gentle and yet very plaintive—not, however, entirely hopeless, as if *Elsa*, being conscious of her innocence, did not despair of her fate. It is chiefly orchestrated for the wood wind instruments, whose soft, smooth, round tones are exactly suited to give expression to the phrases which Wagner has assigned to them. In answer to the *King's* questions *Elsa* inclines her head, and seems with a gesture to say that the accusation is so vile that she can make no answer. Finally she tells the story of her dream in a beautiful melody, while she looks tranquilly before her. Then we hear softly whispered by the violins the

Motive of the Grail, and in dreamy rapture she tells of the knight of glorious mien on whom she gazed. This passage introduces an animated phrase, which occurs again when the knight arrives in answer to her prayers, and is also heard later in the drama. It passes over into a very beautiful melody, broad and flowing, which is subsequently taken up by the chorus. *Frederick*, however, announces his willingness to back his accusation by the ordeal of single combat, and the *King*, turning to *Elsa*, requests her to name her champion. She then proclaims that the knight whom she has seen in her dream shall champion her, and to him whom Heaven shall send she offers her hand in marriage.

The *Herald* steps forth with the four trumpeters, whom he places toward the four points of the compass, the *King* having previously drawn his sword and thrust it into the earth before him. The *Herald* summons *Elsa's* champion to appear, but there is deep silence. Again the trumpets ring out, and now, when there is still no answer, *Elsa*, surrounded by her maids, falls upon her knees in fervent prayer. She has hardly finished before exclamations of wonder from the nobles standing nearest the water call attention to the skiff drawn by a swan which is approaching from a distance. As it draws nearer and nearer the excitement of the beholders finds vent in a wonderfully dramatic chorus composed of detached phrases, which finds, at last, its climax in an outburst of joy as the skiff reaches the bank. *Elsa*, with transported countenance, has remained upon her knees, but now she rises and turns, and, seeing *Lohengrin*, greets him with an exclamation of joy. The excitement gradually gives way to rapt expectancy as *Lohengrin* moves to step out of the skiff. The climax dies away with those long drawn chords which were heard in the prelude, and these are followed by the Grail Motive, which introduces the exquisite farewell to the swan.

The succeeding chorus well expresses the awe which has overcome the assembly at sight of this supernatural champion. *Lohengrin* steps out of his skiff and, making an obeisance to the *King*, greets him. He then converses with *Elsa*, his words being chiefly accompanied by the music familiar from the prelude, he finally putting to her the conditions under which he will champion her cause. Here occurs a phrase of threatful burden, the Motive of Warning, which appears significantly in later scenes. *Elsa* gives herself up entirely to her champion, and he, raising her to his heart, exclaims in a brief but impassioned musical phrase, " *Elsa*, I worship thee ! " The chorus expressive of awe is repeated, and the nobles who stand forth respectively for *Lohengrin* and *Frederick* cross the stage with solemn strides and measure the ground for the combat.

When the six have formed a complete circle, and the *Herald* has warned all not to interfere with the fight, the *King* intones the prayer, which forms one of the most superb numbers in this work. Beginning as a solo for the *King*, it is continued as a quintette, *Elsa, Ortrud, Lohengrin* and *Frederick* joining in it, and then suddenly receives a magnificent impetus from the full chorus, reaching an impassioned and stupendous climax. The *King* draws his sword out of the ground and strikes it three times on the shield that hangs on the oak. With the first stroke *Lohengrin* and *Frederick* step into the circle. With the second they advance their shields and draw ; with the third the combat begins. It is brief and ends with *Frederick's* ignominious defeat, *Lohengrin*, out of pity, sparing his life. The beholders rush to the centre with glad acclamations to hail *Lohengrin* as the victor, and *Elsa* hastens to his side and sings a pæan of joy, which is finally taken up by the chorus and forms a grand finale to this highly dramatic act.

The second act opens with a sombre phrase, interrupted with dramatic significance by the Motive of Warning. The curtain discloses the fortress of Antwerp. At the back is the palace ; in the foreground the dwelling of the women ; to the right the minster. It is night. *Ortrud* and *Frederick*, both in sombre garments, are seated on the steps of the minster. *Frederick* is lost in gloomy thought. *Ortrud* gazes fixedly at the windows of the palace, through which the light is streaming. Sounds of revelry are heard from within.

Frederick arouses himself and bids *Ortrud* follow him in flight ; but *Ortrud* demurs that she is held to the spot by a desire to wreak vengeance upon *Elsa* and her knight. Then *Frederick* in a paroxysm of grief and rage curses his fate in wrathful measures. As he throws himself upon the ground, overcome with anger, festive sounds from the palace are heard again.

Ortrud, with almost fiendish tranquillity, derides him for this violent outburst of temper, and then, with devilish calmness, unfolds to him the plan by which she intends to put an end to the happiness of *Elsa* and her champion. In a weird and sombre incantation, one of the most satanically dramatic passages Wagner has written, they invoke the powers of evil to their aid. This ends the scene between *Ortrud* and *Frederick*, which, at the time the opera was brought out, and even now, is still criticised on account of its unmelodiousness and its length. While perhaps it is, for dramatic purposes, somewhat too long, because what is told therein might be conveyed to the audience in a shorter scene—in fact, the score is now subjected to considerable cutting without at all interfering with the clearness of the story—the episode is undoubtedly one of the most sombrely powerful passages in the whole work. But one can readily understand that when the work was first brought out, some forty years ago, before the operatic public had been fed on leading motives, it must have found this scene pretty tough and indigestible.

After the invocation of the powers of evil the door which leads onto the balcony of the women's apartment opens, and *Elsa* appears in white garments. She steps forward to the parapet and leaning her head upon her hands sings a sweetly melodious strain of gratitude for the sending of her champion. As her voice dies away, *Frederick* disappears to a hiding place,

and *Ortrud* calls in a plaintive voice, "Elsa!" Moved
to pity, *Elsa* hastens down to meet her, and now,
while simulating humility, *Frederick's* wife pours
doubts regarding her champion into *Elsa's* mind, at
the same time moving her to ask for a reprieve for
Frederick. The whole closes with a beautiful duet,
which is repeated by the orchestra as *Ortrud* is conducted by *Elsa* into the apartment. *Frederick* appears
for a moment and hurls his malediction after them.

Trumpets, seemingly sounding from turrets in various parts of the city, now announce the break of
day, and while the warders descend and unlock the
gates, servitors enter from various directions, salute
each other and proceed quietly on their several ways.
Some draw water at the well, knock at the entrance
of the palace and are admitted. The royal trumpeters issue forth from the palace gates and blow the
summons. Nobles and retainers enter and sing a
very spirited chorus, one of the best things in the
work, but usually pretty badly sung, and therefore
rarely achieving its full effect. The *Herald*, whose
frequency is, by the way, somewhat against him, then
announces the decree of exile which has been passed
on *Frederick*, and proclaims that *Lohengrin* is to lead
the host into battle. This is at first hailed with exclamations of joy, but *Frederick* appears and mingling
with the nobles seems to instil them with distrust of
their new captain, and they finally shelter him near
the steps of the minster. The well-known bridal
procession is now intoned by the orchestra, and a
long train of ladies issue forth onto the balcony, de-

scend, pass before the palace, return to the front, and then ascend the steps of the minster, where they remain standing. *Elsa* then appears amid the train, the nobles deferentially baring their heads. *Elsa* reaches the steps of the palace and there she remains standing a while, the chorus singing a song of joy to the melody of the bridal procession. As she places her foot on the second step of the minster *Ortrud*, who until now has been behind the train, hastens forward and savagely confronts her, declaring that she shall have precedence, as *Elsa* cannot even name her champion. She plays upon this inability of *Elsa* to discover the name and race of the knight who has aided her, and *Elsa* is visibly affected.

At this moment, amid flourish of trumpets and acclamations, the *King* appears with *Lohengrin*, and *Elsa* throws herself into his arms. *Lohengrin*, *Elsa* and the *King* turn toward the minster, but here *Frederick* confronts them, charging *Lohengrin* with sorcery, and asking who he is and whence he came, again instilling *Elsa's* mind with doubts. *Lohengrin* turns toward *Elsa*, sees that her bosom is heaving convulsively and that she seems under great emotion. The Motive of Warning rings out again as he chides her ; but after an excited scene the men gather around *Lohengrin* and grasp his hand in token of allegiance. Meanwhile *Frederick* whispers warnings to *Elsa*, until *Lohengrin*, stepping hastily forward bids him and *Ortrud* begone. The bridal procession then proceeds and enters the minster. At the very last moment, before *Elsa* passes through its entrance, she beholds *Ortrud*, who lifts an arm against her with an expression of warning and triumph, and the bride turns away her face in terror.

The third act opens with the brilliant introduction so familiar from concert performances even before the opera itself was ever heard here, and this is followed by the even more famous bridal chorus, which now forms a companion piece to Mendelssohn's "Wedding March" at nearly every wedding ceremony, so that there is probably no tune to whose strains so many people are made happy or miserable. The train which conducted *Lohengrin* and *Elsa* into the bridal chamber having taken its departure we have the exquisite love duet, one of the sweetest and tenderest passages of which the lyric stage can boast. A very beautiful episode is that in which *Lohengrin* points to the open casement, to the flowery close below, softly illumed by the moon, and sings to an accompaniment of what might be called musical moonbeams, "Say, dost thou breathe the incense sweet of flowers?" But in spite of the tender warning which he conveys to her, she begins questioning him. He turns toward her and in a passionate phrase begs her to trust him and abide with him in loving faith; but his words are vain. She dreads that the memory of the delightful place from which he came will wean him from her. In a wild vision she exclaims that she sees the swan approaching to bear him away from her, and then she puts to him the forbidden questions.

This is followed by the attack of *Frederick* and his death, and then there is a dramatic silence during

which *Elsa* sinks on *Lohengrin's* breast and faints.
When I say silence I do not mean that there is a total
cessation of sound, for silence can be more impressively expressed in music than by actual silence
itself. It is done in this case by long drawn out
chords followed by faint taps on the tympani. *Lohengrin* bends down to *Elsa*, raises her and gently places
her on a couch, while echoes of the love duet add to
the mournfulness of the scene. He orders the four
nobles to bear away *Frederick's* corpse and then sig-
nals to the ladies in waiting who are to convey *Elsa*
to the king. The scene closes with the Motive of
Warning, which resounds with dread power.

A quick change of scene is supposed to be made,
but, as a rule, it takes so long that the third act is vir-
tually given in two acts. The next scene opens with
a brilliant march, during which the counts of Brabant
enter on horseback from various directions, followed
by their vassals. There is a vigorous address by the
King ; then *Elsa* and afterward *Lohengrin* enter. *Lohengrin* uncovers the corpse of *Frederick*, which is
borne in, and explains how he slew him, and tells
that he is forced to disclose whence he came, and
then to take leave. *Lohengrin's* narrative is beautifully set to music familiar from the prelude ; but when
he proclaims his name we hear the same measures
which *Elsa* sang in the second part of her dream in
the first act. Very beautiful and tender is the music
which he sings when he hands *Elsa* his horn, his
sword and his ring to give to her brother, should he
return, and also his greeting to the swan when it

comes to bear him back.   After the episodes fully related in the synopsis of the plot, the work is brought
to a close with a repetition of the music of the second
portion of *Elsa's* dream, followed by a superb climax
with the Motive of the Grail.

INDEX TO BIOGRAPHY.

www.ingramcontent.com/pod-product-compliance
Lightning Source LLC
Chambersburg PA
CBHW030110030726
47498CB00007B/2322